The Beautiful Woman Without Mercy

& The King of Scarecrows

Two Novels by

Steven Culbert

BASKERVILLE
PUBLISHERS, INC.
DALLAS • NEW YORK • DUBLIN

BASKERVILLE Publishers, Inc.
7540 LBJ Freeway/Suite 125, Dallas TX 75251-1008

Library of Congress Catalog Card Number: 92-075409
ISBN: 1-880909-02-2

Manufactured in the United States of America
First Printing

To my real parents,
way out West somewhere.

The Beautiful Woman Without Mercy

The drum in a dream
pounds loud to the dreamer.
— Sandburg

Prologue

It was a time when if you had a name you used it, if you didn't you made one up. Or took one. I took *Mott* off a dew-soaked letter I found on a byway by a highway covered with grass. The tragic letter described without much detail how a boy's mother, father and sister, while gathering acorns and pecans near a town called Hugheston, had been caught unbeknownst in the woods at night, and had been harassed through that fateful night and ultimately eaten by wild dogs.

I concluded that perhaps the letter wasn't dew-soaked at all, but tear-soaked. *Mott* was at the torn bottom of the letter, or could be it was followed by a dash at the plain, untorn bottom. In fact, I can't remember.

I figured *Mott* was as good, as workable, as any name, so I took it and it alone I went by for many years. Before, the only other name I had was one my mother gave me, best I can remember, or as I've always held to myself, told myself in moments of nut-hard loneliness along the grassy highway of sleep-alone night . . .

So, anyhow, this is about me and Amy Survivor, a beautiful

woman without mercy, and the band of no-talent bums who followed her around, played her music, and worked on their names—though one guy, the drummer, had the given name *No History*, perfect for a drummer, before he joined the band . . .

This also has to do with a haunted house of pleasure in The Town With No Name; a prairie town called Fate whose name was buried then later dug up by No History scavenging on the outskirts; Jesus Green the Tree Man; the pilgrims of Rag Doll Pass; Banker Bill; Yellow Hat; Jolly Wagoneer; and certain other names given, taken, but ultimately borrowed, which I fail to remember right now or have just forgotten. But first Jesus Green and how I met him.

1

Jesus Green was a kind brown man from the Southern Countries, who sold trees seasonally from the back of a conestoga. Additionally, he was the oldest guy I ever met, which worked out well for me, seeing as how I needed a job about the time we met, with me hitchhiking a ride on the long grass road.

I remember it all, or what I remember, like it was yesterday . . .

Let me back up a little bit. I have two eyes, but one's unusual. It's dead. It's important to know that because it has something to do with the mystery of love the way I know it, and with this business directly . . .

I had been walking for a long, long time along a pretty, narrow byway that skirted the edge of about a tenlane highway covered with grass; the grass was tough and old in its dense, admirable, confused network like a meadow of bermuda mixed with rye in victory. The long highway was a trophy belonging to the vegetation in its contest against oblivion, which it was winning—a contest or war that I guess is still going on.

I'd spent my last night, before meeting Jesus, under a giant old pine tree that lightning apparently had struck or beetles eaten to a certain extent, since its pointed tip hung down like a finger identifying my camping spot about thirty paces to the left.

Like I say, it was a good thing old Jesus came along in his conestoga when he did. I had no idea how close or far away the next nearest town was, and I'd used the last of my nuts on mush the night before. It had been an enjoyable meal, staring up in amazement at a threesome of tender stars over the busted finger of that tree. But there I was on the meadow-road, walking, when I heard that magical sound coming up behind me in the dewy dawn of autumn. I might have smiled, for my pack was light, my earthly burden next to nothing, and the endless grass road covered with nourishment. I'm thinking of the dew. I don't know what a dell is, but I'm sure I was in one. The magical sound was that of a sweet conestoga rolling over the grassy road; when the wind blows just right it's like a memory as it happens.

And even more specially this time, this particular morning, was the sound of Jesus's voice singing an ancient tune, old as the hills: "On a hill far away stood an old rugged cross" and "exchange it some day for a crown" are all the words I can remember. He was singing blindly, I mean, so beautifully, with all his heart, I'm still somewhat surprised the pine tree didn't heal up whole right on the spot.

But that didn't happen. I know because I turned to look. That's exactly when I saw Jesus Green's little horses pulling the wagon. It was full of pine trees, from what I could see of their spars sticking out of the tarp.

I stood and looked at him full face until he stopped and offered me a ride. I wasn't trying to be mean, but just myself. When I got on board I took my pack off and stowed it at my feet. I'd done this a thousand times. Then before I could shake his hand and say thanks, he shocked hell out of me by conjecturing bravely, straight ahead, "Dogbite?"

I figured he was a mystic, sucked snot and spat it out to stall.

"Yep," I said.

He squinted sideways at me, not removing his hands from the reins. He asked if I was hungry, so I discussed my hazelnut mush. He laughed. We shook hands. He told me his life story and offered me a job as his helper unloading and watching his trees in the next town we'd come to, which he called Fate, though there was no sign.

2

He was talking about my dead eye, of course. That's why he looked away from me instead of at me when he talked right at first. As if a dead eye was threatening. But very few people are not that way. Amy Survivor was one. In fact, and I just realized this, no man has ever looked me in the dead eye without faking honesty—except maybe Jesus Green. But I've got to give you something here, and that is that it's hard to tell when people mean what they say, for me, and I dare say this may be true for you. That's one reason not to count on conversation too much. Or at all. And why I write certain things down, like this, where I've no reason to lie.

Anyhow, there was no proof we were approaching a town called Fate, except I did see a post where a sign used to be. I thought, "Somebody ripped it off to burn," which was stupid, because there was wood growing everywhere on the outskirts of Fate. But I nodded off, relaxed because I had a job.

"Nobody's gonna kill you till your job is done," I figured irrationally, once my chin touched my chest.

3

A whip cracked and I woke up in Fate, a collection of wooden buildings one street wide, backed by trees. I'd been there a thousand times, yet it was always new, for which I was thankful. I liked the buildings and knew no inhabitants. That has everything to do reasonably with a desire for loneliness, which sounds crazy and may be true.

We stopped in front of an empty lot beside the biggest building in town, which at one time had been occupied. The lot was full of holes where stakes for big tents had been driven over the years; you could see this by the slant of the holes. Interestingly for me, I jumped off the wagon and right at my feet was a head-splinter off a big stake in the mud. I picked it up just as Jesus yelled, "Unload!"

I took it well. He was a nice guy, and very old, with a job to do. Otherwise he never would have picked me up on the highway. Come to think of it, if he'd never picked me up, I might never have met Amy Survivor. For I have no idea where we went or turned, left or right, or even if we U-turned, after I nodded off.

But I unloaded all the pine trees wrapped in string-like rope and stacked at first apparently haphazard and ultimately with a great deal of care toward the bottom of the conestoga. Underneath all the trees was what Jesus needed all along, a tent. Under the tent—which was both heavy and ancient, as proved by its weight and its rubber, plastic—under the folded tent was a box built into the bed of the wagon, and in the box were splintered stakes. I appreciated that, and felt part of a long tradition.

By the time we had the tent pitched, the sun was all the way up and folks were stepping out of the buildings. They looked across the street at me and Jesus proudly standing pine trees up against steel stakes and tying the trees to them.

I forgot to tell you at the right time about these steel stakes, I guess because they belonged to the property and were not on the wagon, like a sub-tradition. Jesus had found them stacked in a shed fixed against the back of the biggest building in town, and he surprised me with them by carrying them out himself, silently, and not reacting pro or con when I held them still as he hammered them in. Like the buildings and the holes and the wagon and the wooden stakes and Jesus himself, these steel stakes were very old. The tent, too.

After the last stake was driven in and the last pine tree tied to it, Jesus handed me a piece of scrip that read, "Bearer Entitled To Two Hundred Acorns, Twenty Pecans, Eighteen Walnuts, Or Popular Equivalents In Stuff" in Jesus's handwriting, fresh and new. I felt like keeping it, "framing it," as oldtimers used to say. But my stomach growled with a feeling of its own, and a memory of acorn mush rushed to my mind as clear saliva flushed my mouth. I was hungry.

"Need me anymore today?" I asked Jesus.

He said no and told me I could bunk down in the shed behind the biggest building in town.

That's how things were back then. A man helped another, and that's just how it was. When it was sunup, you got up. When it was sundown, you went to bed. With few exceptions. Life was hard, and sleep necessary. That's why, even though it was still early morning, Jesus told me where I could bunk down that night, which meant when the sun went down.

So I went off immediately to dig up some supper, and if not supper itself, something that would turn into supper before nightfall in Fate. It felt good to walk through a strange town with a readymade place to stay, scrip in my pocket, and a job for tomorrow. I guessed I still had a job.

The townsfolk just watched the story unfold, somewhat detached and friendly on wooden porches, while I went looking for a bank to rob.

4

When I say "rob a bank" I mean I went looking for a place to cash my two-hundred-acorn/twenty-pecan note. I'm not a criminal now, nor have I ever been. But, you see, I was feeling good, rake 'n rambling, as the old song used to say, and I was really hungry, which is a good feeling when you know you can do something about it.

I passed through Fate pretty quickly and came to the outskirts of town, where I finally found a bank with your usual guard at the gate. The guard, whom I never met, was somewhat friendly and distant, and he wore a blank name tag. Apparently he had not decided on a name. Or perhaps the tag was for his title. I don't know. Also, he wore a hat like the hat Jesus wore and I forgot to tell you about: a broad-brimmed hat like weird farmers used to wear. Pictures of them, especially paintings, still hang on odd walls, here and there. I don't know what color Jesus Green's hat was originally, but he'd fingered it so much as a nervous habit with sappy treeman's hands and greasy teamster's hands that his hat had become a dark cloud on his old head, the color of a felt tornado formed into a broad hat. On the other hand the guard's hat was better cared for, yellow . . . Additionally, he

carried a gun that must've been in his family for generations, the way it had initials carved in the butt and rested
proudly, or perfectly, on his hip.

This bank was fascinating to me for another thing it had that
was fairly untypical for banks of that region in those times.
That is, it was set up inside a compound of miniature warehouses in rows, identical cubicles in size. You had your own
warehouse if you were rich, and each warehouse had a lock,
the combination to which you owned, so that during bank-
ing hours (sunup to a tad before sundown) you could go in
there and check on your nuts whenever you wanted. I understand people kept other stuff in there, too, but I never did
see any of it.

Anyhow, that region was famous mostly for its great pecan,
oak, and hickory forests—as well as, in the old days, for its
pine—so it was safe to say that the majority of wealth in
those miniature warehouses was nuts.

As with banks just about everywhere, dryness was a top pri-
ority, so on rainy days the bank was shut down and Yellow
Hat got a holiday, with pay. I thought that was fortunate for
him. He looked honest . . .

To get to the point, I marched up to the teller's window, cut
into the side of the warehouse, and knocked on the shutter
(the glass had been broken, who knows how long ago, and
the hole was covered with shutters).

The teller who opened the window looked like a puppet.
That's the best way to describe him as he smiled out at me
within the light of an oil lamp. I believe peanut oil was

burning, which was wasteful, considering the day was not rainy or dark.

To my surprise he extended his hand to greet me. I shook it and handed him my note. That's when the fun started. For me. I told him it was not a deposit.

"Acorns or pecans?" he asked.

"Acorns, please."

Then, as he turned stiffly and limped on a bum leg toward a door in the shadows behind him, I changed my mind:

"No. Make that one hundred acorns and ten pecans, please."

He never changed expression.

5

Besides the nuts, these are the things I had in my pack: a nutcracker, a picture purported to be of my mom and dad (ripped), a pocket-size combination book of wisdom and dictionary which I carried for culture but barely consulted, a second shirt like a fancy or on-the-town shirt, a pencil, a deerskin pouch of special spices I used in mush on special occasions (as later with Amy Survivor), a very impractical glistening rock I found on the road way south on a lucky day and kept because of that, another pair of woolly pants I wore only when doing laundry because otherwise they scratched like hell and were no good for walking, matches, an ancient timepiece of partial gold, a picture of a beautiful girl, a hickory wood nut-masher hard as rock and barely worn down in its waffled face (so useful) after years of use (got for trade, fifty walnuts, up North), a hickory wood bowl out of which I ate and in which I prepared to eat what things I earned and gathered.

Otherwise I had nothing. No secrets. In those days, any man with strength to get down on all fours could drink right off the ground, or out of any stream, or milk a cow for wages. I fancied a pair of buckskin pants and thought to save up and get a pair someday but, hell, I wasn't rich. That'd take more pecans than one man, one good man working hard every day, could gather in a winter. As for my slick wool pants, the road pair I got tremendous use of, I didn't even know how old they were, or whose they were first.

I guess I do have certain secrets. I shaved with my knife, but never had much of a beard. I remember looking in a puddle to shave and seeing geese fly over before I heard them in the harsh wind, a while before meeting Jesus Green and coming to Fate. I really don't remember when. That kind of mystical stuff is hard to place in time.

This is getting us nowhere. I'm worn out just trying to place events in some kind of logic you can use and take with you. I had a hundred acorns and ten pecans in a complimentary paper bag the bank furnished as a come-on to make future deposits there, in my pack now, too.

6

I spent some time in a combination of goofing off and exploring the terrain around Fate when I looked up and discovered it was high noon. The sun was a polka dot in a gray nightgown. I'd seen one once, on a saloon woman way up North when I was extremely young, an early memory.

Anyway, I'd wasted most of the day sleeping in the roots of a star magnolia that bridged a creek. I felt like a tiny thing nestled in hair blown up a billion times its size, just sawing logs. I had a dream I don't remember. Other things occurred. I saw various animals. A deer. Pill bugs. Moss. Sleep. Sleep's an animal that eats you up slowly. Its lips are very soft and its teeth are very hard. I've observed as most animals get older they sleep more and are less willing to rise. That takes for granted you can see how things are.

The deer was very old, a buck. I tend to see velvet horns. Antlers like Jesus Green's trees. He meandered up the creek ravine toward me as I slept on my arm and opening my eyes I saw him go to his knees, then drop to his haunches and nibble-nuzzle grass at a rock washed over a million years when it rained. When I woke up finally he was gone.

But I still had to eat. I peered up through the roots of the magnolia and wondered how I'd eat my acorns and pecans, with or without spices, raw, or heated on rocks. That's the kind of thing I used to think over when I found myself with time on my hands. I also thought about women, fishing, and my family, though I'd never been fishing in my life and my folks and sister were mostly just made-up memories.

So I forced myself suddenly to get practical. I sat up. I relapsed into sleep and had a dream of a naked girl I'd never seen before. I woke up in the roots of that big star magnolia and realized the pressure was on. I jumped up, slung my pack, and climbed out to the surface. That's when I looked up through the still green branches of the mighty star magnolia and saw the polka-dot sun set in the gray nightgown of a saloon-girl who may never have existed. But she was part of me, and a good part, too, however she got that nightgown.

I made town in a matter of minutes and in doing so crossed over a sizable creek with no sign naming it. Without stopping, I was mystified as to how I hadn't seen this creek the first time out. The creek was fully lined with trees thick as hair and nearly inaccessible, by appearance. Fate lay up ahead, its wooden buildings. I could see it.

7

In Fate I heard a child cry in a house along the wood side-walk that stretched up and down the only street in town. It cried "Mama." I felt a twinge of something that wasn't hunger, but buried under hunger, and hefted my pack higher on my shoulders, in full stride toward a hot meal. This I would find but I didn't know where. I could have gone back to my place and crushed a bowl of nuts. But I didn't. Fatefully, I didn't want to be alone at sundown, and I figured, in a town this size there had to be a nut house where, for a handful of pecans, a man could get a hot meal and a hot cup of tea.

It was getting wintry in the afternoon ablaze with red and yellow leaves falling down and turning brown before my very eyes. I started fantasizing about honey logs when there it was, on a little sign freshly painted on a piece of plywood old as the hills, buckled and splintered but no doubt the best they could do: Nut House. Not terribly new, but a useful name for a nut house. It left no doubt in your mind.

It felt weird to walk in and be inside a house for the first time in a long time. The place was empty of people. A little sign, painted on plywood again, ordered those entering Nut House to remove hats and packs. It was that kind of place. Real homey, but all business.

I took the first table by the door and waited for someone to come out. No one did. I got tired of waiting. Some leaves blew up against the door, and I got up to leave. But it was too late, because a girl walked in blustery through the charming door just as I opened it to leave in disappointment. Happily, I sat back down at my table, though she completely ignored me. I sat there for a long time as I hoped for her to come back out. All I heard, though, was her rumbling around in back. I couldn't even smell a nut-house hot meal special cooking, which at times in my life I'd prayed for, just the smell, on coming into strange towns. No. Nothing.

I crossed my arms over my chest, and crossed my legs under the table, and dozed off. That was better than hammering on the poor old table.

I woke up to her walking away from me through rising steam like a ghost over the nut-house special: blueberry cobbler. I said, "Thanks," but she must have not heard me, or if she did, she walked back into the back and didn't respond. I didn't mind. I ate a hot meal fit for a king.

When I finished, she came out with a pot of hot tea for me to have after supper, and put it on the table. Somehow I already felt it was mine, my table, my pot of tea.

What a joke. She never cracked a smile. I got up to pee and asked her where to go. She didn't answer again and I went out the back door, naturally, to pee.

When finished I couldn't get back in. The back door was locked. I thought it was a mistake. I walked around front and found the front door locked, too. Then it struck me. It was night. I'd slept a long time, waiting for a hot meal and a bitter look. I should have looked outside and paid more attention to the world at large. But I didn't. That was water down river.

Anyhow, my belly was full. I'd got what I needed. Amazed how that will happen again and again, something dawned on me: "My pack's in there." And it was. I thought for a minute I'd been had. Then I knocked gently on the door and nobody answered. I knocked a little harder. Nobody. I pounded on the door and nobody answered. It was night, after all. I knew better.

8

I thought about it this way. My pack containing all my worldly possessions except the clothes on my back, my wool pants and moccasins, was too much to pay for a nut-house special. I stood there in total darkness because there was no moon and it was cloudy again, and wondered what in this world I would do if she had stolen my pack. I didn't even know her name.

I sighed and looked down the one street of Fate toward the biggest building in town, behind which I knew at least I had a place to stay. But it was too dark to see. You couldn't see your hands in front of your face. I imagined how pitch dark it must have been in my secret place under the star magnolia. Then someone grabbed my arm. Whoever it was had the advantage. It was Jesus Green, the treeman.

I told him the whole story. He said, "Figures." I said, "How?" We walked out in the middle of the street so as not to bump into anything, about ten paces, before he answered that Amy Survivor was deaf. Gosh, I felt awful bad about doubting her original intentions. Calling in your mind a deaf girl a thief. Even if it's true, nobody should care.

My mind was full of these personal thoughts. It felt good to be there in the wide open spaces of the main street of Fate, with Jesus Green, a job tomorrow, a place to stay (inside), and a reason to return to the Nut House for breakfast. For one thing, Amy Survivor was damn good looking. For another, she could sure bake a mean nut-house cobbler. Those are two fine traits in a person, hard to take away.

Then I thought of something. I asked Jesus if Amy Survivor could talk. Looking at the ground, I guess because I was, he said something intriguing, a perfect finish to my first evening in Fate. He said he never got close enough to know.

From that point on we walked in silence. I learned why later on. Scribbled on the back of a twenty-pecan note Jesus gave me, in his own handwriting, was the motto: "Between loose talk and silence, opt for silence."

It must have been his idea. I never found it in any book of wisdom.

9

We passed through the smell of pines. Jesus Green's trees were blacker than night and pointed to invisible stars like ghosts chained to posts. Of course Jesus hoped someone would buy them and take them away before the time would come when their lives were just wasted. Why else would a man be in the tree business? An old man?

Jesus produced a key from somewhere and unlocked a padlock locking shut the tin door of the tin shed affixed to the back of the biggest building in Fate; still, my heart sank as he undid the top half of the lock from the bottom half, lifted it off the latch of the tin door, and the door opened.

We walked in and Jesus struck a match on the ceiling and for the first time I saw where I'd live while I worked for Jesus Green. In a flash I saw a little bed they call a twin but there was only one, a black stove tiny with a pipe to the ceiling, to my left a picture eerie in its frame, to my right above the bed a small window standard size and painted over a color I couldn't tell. The floor was dirt, to my satisfaction. No matter how cold, nothing on a floor feels as good. This may be true only to me of all the people of the world, all the rovers who live off the fat of the land, as the old saying goes—but I doubt it. Others must feel this way. Other rovers. I didn't care. I just wanted Jesus to leave so could slip off my moccasins and enjoy it.

I guess Jesus trusted me. He handed me the key to the place and showed me where further matches were stored in a box marked "Decorator" on a ceiling beam. His match went out, extinguished in the callus of his thumb, it seemed, just as he held it to the crossbeam above the door to show me the traditional-bend eye-hook where the key was hung by those living there in season. Luckily it was a long match; elsewise I wouldn't have seen as much as I did, in all the excitement of going to bed after a long day's roving around and with no bad feelings harbored against anybody in the whole yearning world.

Without striking another match, Jesus left and I stood wrapped in dark-time as the tin door shut behind him. I stood quietly to hear what I could hear, for a considerable moment. Trees wished in wind I heard through blackest shadows where the tin roof met the tin sides, the whole thing waving. I noticed the walls and all were waved with that time-honored, rolled effect of tin buildings since way back when.

I felt for the bed with my foot and found it immediately. The whole shed wasn't six paces across. I sat on the bed with my moccasined feet flat on the floor and took off my moccasins. Ah.

10

I woke up in the middle of the night and struck a match to find a blanket because I was cold. Odd how I figured there'd be one there, and there was. I'd slept in my clothes and moccasins, but winter was coming down, and it wasn't enough. The wind blew hard enough to carol in the eves. There were some mouse turds in the blanket, but only a few, dry and old. Another sign of life was a mockingbird song that sputtered off and on as the wind blew suddenly harder, then died off. I hoped the mocker had a nest in the howling stovepipe, but couldn't count on it. I figured I'd be out of there before the winter truly came and could leave the stove to the bird, unharassed. He'd be in the pipe, happy.

Wrapped up tighter than a papoose in the borrowed blanket, I had other thoughts I don't remember, but one dream of an ancient moviehouse containing a spotty audience of both sullen and chuckling people (I was a chuckler) watching a man on the fuzzy screen read what they used to call "the news," I believe. I remember one excerpt. The speaker told of wild dogs breeding in the wombs of women. I took it to be a joke. As I laughed I turned to see who else was laughing; nobody was. Their fang-ripped faces gaped in bloody belief. Oddly I woke up laughing from the dream but, judging by the way I felt, sweaty and shaky, determined it was a nightmare. Again oddly, odder, I went back to sleep, hoping to return to the moviehouse to see who they were, but, ultimately, just fell asleep . . .

It was still dark when I woke up for the day. You know how that feels. I wouldn't go back to sleep. I would just lie on the bed and wait for daylight. A knock came to my door just as I was rebuilding the elements of the moviehouse dream and about to drift back asleep despite my intentions. I woke up like a drunk man feeling his wine yanked from his hands, then went to the door. It wasn't even locked. If they wanted me, they couldn't have just come in. Maybe Jesus needed matches to start his coffee. He had his own. Mine were his. I was hired help. Thoughts like that. More or less silly, drunken thoughts. However, I could not recall ever being drunk enough to think screwed up.

Outside the door was a basket wrapped in an ancient cloth, red and white checkered. I hoped there wasn't a baby in it. (Isn't that foolish?) I looked around to see if anybody saw me wrapped in the blanket. Of course, I had my moccasins on. They'd know I wasn't naked. It was just getting light. I jerked up the basket quick and it was heavy. It couldn't be a baby. Mystified and finally awake, I went inside and shut the door behind me, this time slipping the padlock through the latch but not snapping it shut.

I set the basket on the bed and sat down beside it. Gently, I lifted the cloth and looked inside. Jellies, jams, mincemeat in ancient bottles; an acorn loaf big as your head, and a pecan patty of solid big pecans, broad as both my hands put together.

Who would do this? I thought. Who even knows I'm here? Far as I could tell, Jesus wasn't married. He wore no ring. I had seen the sparse provisions in his wagon. Walnut shells at the wagoneer's feet.

I felt very thankful, and decided not to eat this stuff right now, but wait till later. In that regard, I was glad it was getting cooler day by day. It never dawned on me till later that day, watching Jesus's trees, that it might've been Amy Survivor.

11

I folded my blanket to keep the mice out of it (as it was getting winter, they'd be coming in), and put it on my bed. Then I stowed my welcome basket under my bed, combed my hair with my fingers, and headed to work. I didn't lock my door, hoping to find the owner of the basket come back to get it when I popped in at noon to check things out, as is my wont when I have a job and a place to stay. The basket was very old, large, and lovely. Willow. It barely fit under my bed.

By the time I got to Jesus under the tent, the tree lot was already crowded with the townsfolk of Fate. They milled around the pines like there was no tomorrow. They had to get a tree. I honestly think every person in Fate was there, and weaving in and out of those pines before I even got my lazy butt to work. Jesus handed me a mug of hot coffee. I took it. He didn't seem to mind that I was apparently late. Maybe he was happy. I stood there for a minute like I owned the place, holding my mug of steaming brew.

The fact he had real coffee indicated just how much Jesus Green had been around. I stood sort of in awe of him, to think of his experience in life. As I've already reported, he was the oldest man I'd ever met or seen, whichever I said. Somehow, though, he was tough and green, and thus his perfect name.

A child was singing a carol from long, long ago, no doubt picked up from her parents, as they were quite old and their parents probably dead. It was a beautiful thing to hear, there in the pines. In fact, the courageous little girl went so far as to pick out her own tree for her little family, even trying to untie the tree from its earthly stake of steel. It was almost enough to make a grown man cry.

I ultimately helped her untie the tree, for she appeared on the verge of panic, her little red fingers slaving at the knot that Jesus had tied the day before. It was pitiful, but she was courageous. I can honestly say I loved her and would have died for her. Jesus seemed undistracted as he took the acorns from her dad. It could be he hadn't seen her trial or heart. On the other hand, he'd probably seen this little girl a thousand times. But I just can't believe it. How often do you see a person you'd die for? I asked myself as the father hauled the tree away by the bleeding trunk, his daughter holding the starry tip. I don't know where the mother was.

I'll tell you how much I was affected: I wondered if Jesus was blind to human love and operated supernaturally to find his way in the dark, to get to be so old yet remain energy-filled and ambitious and all. Then it dawned back on me his kindness in giving me a job, place to stay, and twenty-pecan note in his own writing for no reason at all but half a morning's work. He could have unloaded those pines and set up the tent alone. I'm sure he had many times before he picked me up on that grassy highway. Funny, how a little girl can affect you.

Jesus elbowed me and said, "Don't look." The fact that I scalded my hand mattered not. Somehow that was the case, as I looked and there came Amy Survivor in a fancy dress older than the hills, the color of the sky that morning, a matchless pure blue, and with her four guys carrying instruments of various sorts: a hollow-log drum carried by a short, stocky guy; a mountain box with very ancient strings (I only found out later as I heard them struck) carried by a skinny, hound-dog-looking guy with hair like Amy Survivor's, a wild woman's hairdo; a flute packed in a battered ancient case by a tiny fellow in a black suit, who smiled nervously; and a stringed box, a homemade instrument from all appearances, carried by a weirdly handsome type with real-combed, not finger-combed hair, a troubadour type I'd seen on the trail. Somehow, the name *womanizer* comes to mind.

Strangely, they sat down in the middle of the main street of Fate and started to play. It sounded, frankly, terrible. They played sincerely and with all their hearts and skill. Veins popped out in their foreheads and necks. Their fingers plied, plucked and quivered. No matter, though. They couldn't play. They were learners. Nobody threw them acorns.

Amy Survivor just sort of sat in the midst of them, like the center of a lopsided circle, their pivot or inspiration. She wove her pretty head of wild woman hair in easy circles with her eyes gently shut, as if she could hear the music. Fact is, however, the stocky drummer sat near her, just behind, beating hell of out of his log with his stubby fists. He was the only one who could play. That, I figured, was better than nothing.

Jesus smiled as he turned to his work selling trees. Me, I stood with the rest of Fate, staring at the bad music better than no music. Oak, hickory, and pecan leaves blew down main street and across Amy's face. She swept them away like the kisses of angels she didn't need. She moved her lips to the song she couldn't hear or really sing. I half-wondered what Jesus had meant by his warning. I could hear his smile like a sound. But I didn't care. I had this.

12

I guess I shouldn't have had that coffee. Otherwise I wouldn't have seen things that weren't there. Or maybe I would have. But I saw what I saw. Who knows, besides her, what she saw? I get tired fast of thinking about that. Other things began bothering me from that moment when I saw the Amy Survivor Band playing in the dirt road, on. They have to do, one and all, with mixed company. I was just a rover with a dead eye till I saw her. I even forgot about my worldly belongings as I assisted Jesus in setting up new trees and selling the old that morning after seeing her in broad daylight.

I forgot about noon, till Jesus told me, pointing at the sun, to break for lunch. I went directly to my shack behind the biggest building in town, which of course was there on the tree lot. The basket was gone. It must have been Amy. It had to be. Nobody else even knew me, much less where I lived. Who else knew what I needed? Who else had a reason? The Welcome Wagon was ancient history even before Mott was a name on that tear-soaked letter of terror from whence I took my name. Also, she might have felt bad about shutting me out of the Nut House the way she had. Even though it had been dark, I was a strange rover in town. She should have known! She could have lit a lamp and set it on my table by the door and hung back in silence in the darkness of the Nut House till I needed her. Right?

No. I know better now and I knew better then. Things happen in this life that have nothing to do with anything. Jesus drank that coffee day and night, and he never changed. He treated me like family, near as I can tell. He was always the same man. People flocked to the lot to buy those trees. They weren't his or anybody's. He never claimed they were. Things happen we can't explain. I'm guessing. I'm roving.

The jellies, jams, mincemeat, bread and patty were ranged along a beam of the ceiling. A slim beam of sun snuck in around the stove pipe and lit the jelly purple. Grape, I figured. Certain things can be figured from facts. Names can be stolen. In so doing, little is missing. When I took an early bite off that pecan patty, it was essentially gone forever. That's important only in that I'd miss it later, as I'll try to remember to tell you when the time comes. Moreover, the ceiling was definitely low enough for her to reach it on tiptoe . . .

I pinched off a bit of the patty and set it in the corner of the shack, under a spider web, hoping that if the mice came back for the winter that day while I was out, they'd get suckered by the piece and leave the whole patty up on the beam unexplored. Then I went back to work, having burned up most of my lunchtime, I figured, with senseless thought, pointlessness. And there were the pines, all pointed.

13

When quitting time rolled around it was almost dark. Those short winter days felt like they were here, though this was only one day in my life and it wasn't winter yet. But it would be. And I missed my pack, my worldly belongings, the way a man misses such things. Well, for one thing, all my nuts were in it and without them I had no way either to fix supper or purchase it. Moreover, I knew Jesus wouldn't pay me again for several days, or suspected he wouldn't pay me until he felt like it.

Fact is, and was, I'm not the kind of guy to ask for pay before the time comes. Jesus paid me that first day either out of the goodness of his heart or because he saw a one-eyed drifter with no money on a grass-covered highway and figured I needed it. Or both. He was right, I guess. But I figure, a dead eye in your head is better than no eye, an empty socket. I've seen that, and I prefer my condition.

On the other hand, I don't believe it helped my tree salesmanship. I think people are more afraid than pitiful of my eye. Through time I've come to understand or just accept this. It no longer bothers me, except when old people who are beyond it look at me and cry, or when little kids scream as I smile at them on the street or in nut houses. That hurts. But, like I said, I'm used to it. Somehow it has never affected my confidence, if I have any. No one has ever told me I have, but I must, the way I just get up and go and face the grassy road whenever and wherever I like. It's my way, I guess.

On the other hand, how do I know? For example, that day, when Jesus Green yelled out "Quittin' time" like he had forty men working for him, and I just headed immediately straight for the Nut House to fetch my pack, which may not have been there, and walked right in like I owned the place and up to the jams and jellies counter and rapped on its smooth ancient oak wood with my knuckle, was it hunger, desire, or confidence that drove me to take drastic action? Looking back on it now, I think Jesus was rubbing off on me. But, really, I don't know. It could have been my own nature coming out, at nightfall . . .

Mysteriously, there wasn't a soul there. Also, at the moment I'd walked off the lot, it was day, and at the moment I turned to leave the Nut House an empty-handed fool, it was night. Because it wasn't more than two hundred paces of one yard average each from the lot to the Nut House, this experience is doubly odd in memory as it comes back now.

But all was not hell. When I set about gathering acorns illegally in the woods near Fate, a thick forest that in fact ebbed right up to the alley that skirted behind my shed and every other building along the only street in town, which I'll call Main Street, though it really had no name except a buried name, like that of the town itself, I came across Amy Survivor under a massive cottonwood, as if a woman, or a man, could find food there. She was smiling and looked weird in a gossamer gown, all alone, until I came, with not a moon or star to keep her company. It was overcast so the sky looked like grease with hints of glitter in it hidden, afloat and cold without anything to do with anybody, to speak anything of, and nothing to do with acorns.

I bring up acorns in this context because I needed them. I don't know why I didn't just head back to my house after the Nut House experience and there eat part of my big acorn loaf. I can only suppose, now, so far in the future, that I was packratting foodstuffs for colder days.

With nothing on my mind, and surprised to find her there, I bore witness to the dreamy fact that Amy Survivor had a light all her own. In her gossamer she fairly glowed. She opened the top of her gown and tucked between her silver breasts were nuggets of little acorns she had gathered for me, I figured out later. For then, as I stood amazed, cold and hungry as the sky or the dim stars in it, I just saw the nourishment I needed, a shadowy fruit.

14

Nothing I have ever had in my life tasted better than the bread Amy made from those acorns warmed by the cockles of her heart and later crushed, rolled, and maneuvered into a little loaf she baked in the old black stove in my hut. It seems impossible now, all the beauty and softness. But my memory was fed, and it remains. Beauty and tenderness rolled up into one ball of a loaf I ate. That was the *it* I was after, that ended up costing me a lot, eating my heart in return. That was the meat of the nut, fair trade. That was the eat-and-be-eaten law I knew. I have no argument.

Thing is, I had nothing on my mind as I watched her work in the dark. My shack or hut or shed, as you like, was fairly warmed by the fire in the stove, but it was yet quite dark. I heard no peep from the mockingbird I had hoped was there. The wind stood still. Atop the stove, on a black lid, Amy made warm tea of leavings she pulled like a weirdness from a hidden pocket of her gossamer gown . . .

Oh, she was so wan and wild and silent! I figured the quietude due to her deaf mute nature. This is how it was: I felt I was in the den of a deaf and dumb fairy princess who knew the spells of a lawless world.

It was getting on winter outside the walls of my house, but there was a weird harvest within. The tea tasted of tranquility and misery, like death. On my bed Amy stared down on me and smiled with her opening mouth as her squirrel eyes blackened in haze. I shut my eyes and imagined her wings as she flew through hell and made the angels sigh.

You know the story that's old as the hills, or older. She drew it out, fueling me on tea, and when the first light came she was boiling more. Only after falling asleep and waking up in the twin bed with her not there, did I permit myself a morsel of bread.

I walked outside and saw that it was a bit past noon and pretty quiet, still, for a town like Fate, with people in it. Rounding the biggest building in town, I found no tent, no trees. Jesus was gone. I figured he had sold all his trees as I slept. I hated that for a moment, then felt better as I realized I wouldn't have to feel bad by looking him in the eyes to explain.

I walked into the street and thought I picked up the smell of horses on the breeze, but it was manure on my moccasins. Shit and leather. I laughed and felt better, like Jesus had done it on purpose. Then, honestly, I sighed, remembering the good two days I'd had with him. The pitiful girl carrying the tree with her father, poor angel.

Yet the terror came to know how sweet she was. The silken sheen of an acorn hull was the squirrelly scream of her eyes. But an emptiness of meat having been was not mine then. I bore no story. My heart had been drained of pluck; my mind had nothing in it as I walked shit-heeled down toward the Nut House to see if my worldly possessions were there.

15

I scraped my feet on the worn old edge of the wooden side-walk that fronted the Nut House and every other building up and down main street, Fate. Then I knocked on the door and nobody answered. I knocked on a nut house door as if it were somebody's house, and it wasn't. I guess I thought Amy lived there. She didn't. Then I wised up and tried to open the door like a patron. It was locked, fortunately, for I realized how foolish I would look if there were people in there, after I had been standing on the sidewalk, knocking.

All this was happening since Amy Survivor fed me that tea and loaf and herself. Still, I needed my pack back.

I walked around the side of the Nut House and tried the side door, which had probably never been used. When I turned the handle it creaked loud enough to wake the whole town of Fate, which by the way had not yet made a peep that fateful day. I say "fateful," but what day isn't, after falling in love with a . . . girl like Amy Survivor?

Around back, in the woody alley cool as the belly of a forest, with the woods a few paces away, I knocked on the back door, but nobody answered. I sighed, and beat on the door. Nobody answered.

"Amy!"

It felt just like the other night, before my dignity was lost along with my other worldly possessions. Momentarily, I decided not to burgle the Nut House for a pack full of all I owned, and instead doubled back quick to my shed to see what I could salvage.

Luckily, the place was not locked. Rather, it was just how I left it. It felt so good to see things just as they had been. So much had happened since falling asleep and waking up to find Jesus gone and Fate asleep. I guessed it might not have been love, but evil that had trapped me. On the other hand, I was crazy tired, as if I'd worked selling pines all day and night with no sleep.

I ate about half the acorn loaf off the rafter, thinking that perhaps Amy Survivor had not baked it after all, then lay down to sleep till I woke up naturally on my bed.

What a glorious feeling. Eyes closed, I turned my face toward the shed's main light source, the window painted black, and something cut my cheek. It was a jackknife open on the bed, with a new twenty-pecan note in Jesus Green's hand pegged on the blade.

I guess he figured, with its black handle of ancient bone greased with time, I'd never see it if the blade wasn't opened. I was lucky it didn't stick my eye.

I checked the knife for carvings engraved on it, but found none. I figured there might be the initials J.G. cut in the bone, but figured wrong. I couldn't know why, yet.

It was on the back of that note I saw the motto I tried to match up with sayings in the book of wisdom, and couldn't. I did that with tired eyes and a cut cheek that bled actually very little.

As I say, it could have been my eye on the blanket. My good eye. Though, when I sleep, I feel both eyes close; I don't mean blink, I mean close for rest. The dead eye needs rest, too.

17

The way he stared wasn't natural. Not a whisker flinched. I stared so hard I could see waverings in his eyes caused by the waverings of the now hearty blaze in the stove. I guess you've seen mouse eyes in firelight: onyx pinheads. But having them fixed on you—tender, pitiful, courageous—is hard to take. It was hard to go to sleep. There might have been other mice just as brave, just as hungry. A rover alone thinks crazy things when his worldly pack has disappeared and a mouse is staring him down. That's not just loose talk. You may just know what I mean.

It got to me, after a while. I decided to figure out what made the bastard tick. So I got up naturally, and stepped up to him, about one pace, to right under his rafter. He looked like a decoration on half a hat. His frozen eyes followed me. He didn't budge.

"Who are you?" I said.

It is my wont to talk to animals so as to put us on even ground. Sometimes it works. I'll make it easy if I can. But he said nothing. Not a squeak. Then it dawned on me maybe he was so scared of me, a burglar to him, he was scared stiff, as in that old saying.

I decided to shake him out of it and shouted "Hey!" in his face.

I thought a whisker twitched. It could have been my own moustache. Once it had happened you never knew. Too much detail. Things got fuzzy when you got too close and I was beyond too close, and should have known. Too close, too late, too much, I took the bait and charge of the moment, and quick as a cat I fingered his head.

See, if I had fingered his nose, he might have bit me dead (an old wives' tale). But sadly he didn't move. He was dead. Suddenly it all made sense. How else could a rodent find the guts to stare a man down?

With a sense of relief I stoked up the fire as preparation to think things through. Mainly I wanted my pack back and to see Amy Survivor again. I figure anybody might know why, because once you get a taste of that tea, you go back for more, naturally. Then thinking of that tranquility and misery, like death, I thought in turn about the mouse and how he died. It dawned on me that if it was the acorn bread that killed the mouse, either he ate too much, too fast, or it was poisoned.

Could the shock of Amy's ghost have killed it? Possible. That's one of those things you never know until it's too late to tell about—years later after everything has calmed down and all the mice haunting the stolen or borrowed shacks of the past are really dead, and their offspring have taken over.

Anyhow, I had real blessings to count as I warmed first

front, then back, by the stove. I had my mind and health, the clothes on my back, a new jackknife I never earned (free as a gift), a twenty-pecan note Banker Bill would take even with a hole in it, and my latest acquisition: a picture of a steel buggy dating back to the big panic where people dashed out hysterically and buried everything, their worldly possessions, in the hope of saving some, according to the wives' tale.

So, as is my wont, I tucked the picture under my arm and, having made my move already in my mind, I left, stuffing the mouse into my pocket for good measure, without actually ever knowing why or caring a whole lot.

18

Because starlit, the street of Fate was not so dark. I could see certain things very clearly as shadows and shapes, none moving, down the silver ribbon of Main Street through the black hair of town. With no lights on earth, we still have stars. I believe that and know that, and always have, down inside, without telling anybody. In fact, the memory of stars is better than the stars themselves as they explode and waste, shooting for something. Sometimes I think stars are early learners come out at night to see.

I saw no earthly sight down the main street of Fate till I got to the edge of town. That's when I saw Yellow Hat approaching, carrying a lantern in the spirit of the season. He saw me as a shadow walking toward him, I guess, and shouted "Stop!" officially. I put two and two together and realized he was doubling as town constable at night, bank guard by day.

"Okay," I shouted, and stopped.

I supposed the worst in situations like this, and figured he made me out a criminal. A good, respectable town cop, he refrained from drawing his gun.

I waited for him to reach me at the end of the main street of Fate, which seemed twenty paces boldly, officially taken. It was kind of exciting till he held his lantern up to my face and asked me where I got "that picture," which was also when I saw his big hat and sidearm.

"What are you doing with that?" he said.

Caught redhanded I did one of the stupidest things I've ever done in my life. I dropped the painting. It hit the dirt of Main Street like a shovel. He picked it up and said, "Come with me," and I did.

We walked side by side, out of town, the way I was headed anyway, toward the warehouse bank. Caught redhanded, as I say, with no way out, I just relaxed. I had a good feeling about Yellow Hat, and, in fact, remembered back to the day I first met or saw Amy Survivor, which was the day I first met Jesus Green and he and I had walked side by side, like constables, back to the lot. It was a good experience, not altogether repeatable.

The cherry on the muffin was seeing that yellow-white human light shining in the guardhouse window, a four-paner. Yellow Hat unlocked the guardhouse door and stuck my painting in there. I knew I'd never get it back and that it wasn't mine to begin with. I figured it would someday find its original home, since Fate was not a big town, and Hat could check through all the buildings for a faded square on a wall the exact size of the painting in his spare time at night. That would give him something to do with his lantern if there weren't any rovers in town.

I felt pretty good till he unlocked a metal warehouse at the far end of a lane of warehouses from Banker Bill's window, or where it was when open; locked, the wretched clerk's window looked like a cut in the wall, with a padlock on it as big as your fist.

But I laughed to myself, and grinned in the dark of the tin warehouse, knowing as I had already known for years, that if somebody wanted to take something from you, they would. A lock couldn't keep them out.

I felt okay till Yellow Hat slammed the tin door behind me, and locked it, keeping the key.

19

The vault had no window, so I stood in utter darkness. Though somewhat disoriented in the strange place I had yet grown used to such, for being a rover so long. Also, I wasn't entirely unprepared for the odd moment, and felt no despair, for I had stolen not only the painting from my last place to stay, but also a fistful of strike-anywhere matches that found a quick way off their old rafter to my other pants pocket opposite the mouse.

Soon as Yellow Hat's key left the padlock of my prison (a bank) and I heard his last bootsteps die away, I struck a match off my thumbnail, since I was sure of that surface and wouldn't waste a valuable match experimenting on the heel of my moccasin.

With firelight I felt better. For one thing, you can see things in firelight. An added feature with firelight is its warmth and utility: it can catch. In times of hunger past I'd lit campfires and rolled up asleep with snares set around trees near the outskirts of the campfire light. By morning I'd had a curious critter for breakfast. But, for all I know, it was luck that brought them, or my smell.

After gathering grub hither and yon off the fat of the land
for long enough you get what rovers of old called the *opti-
mum smell.* You don't smell as human as you do around
women. Whether true of women, too, I can't avouch, for
I've never known a female rover, though I have seen two.

They were two old women, with little moustaches and
stranded goatees they tucked in their shirts to hide as I approached and passed hauling firewood in very young youth
long ago. They primped and giggled, wild as hell, as I
passed their semi-permanent campsite cluttered with unnec-
essary relic clothing, ancient and battered, falling apart like
berry-dyed milkweed, hung on trees round about.

I'd smelled their pot of Old Sock (walnuts and gooseberries
in a jam) from a mile at least down trail, and fantasized
stopping for a bowlful, but no way. They taunted me by
primping and offering long spoons of the Old Sock, a
rover's delicacy surpassed only by sweet squirrel; but I
couldn't stop. They were undoubtedly lonely old hags, and
pitiful, but I couldn't afford, at that time, to lose the rover's
odor I had built up. Animals were less afraid of me than
ever before. I could live fairly easily off the fat of the land
anywhere I roved. One night with a woman would blow it
all, everything I'd worked toward and waited months to ob-
tain. Besides, they were too frightening, and at that time I
had no beard at all to speak of and would feel at a strict dis-
advantage. I skipped it . . .

Back to now.

In the warehouse vault on the verge of winter in the town of
Fate I struck a match and saw immediately Yellow Hat's

53

mistake, for he had jailed me in a cell packed to the ceiling with pecans, walnuts, hazels and *almonds!* These were not the penny-ante acorn or the impossible Brazil. No, Yellow Hat had stupidly, I'm sure, jailed me in Fate's main vault!; he'd put a redhanded thief rover adrift but jailed in a ware-house of his main desire. Also, not a pace away from where I stood awestruck with a burning kitchen match were stacked colorful blankets of the woolen make.

Then an odd thing happened, to show you how history works. I burnt my thumb and before I could get set to strike another match, I started to shiver. In the darkness of a one-eyed rover when the lights go out I discovered it was suddenly winter, too. This happens. I've heard others speak of it. Winter was upon me and I had food, shelter, and cloth-ing in abundance to last me the long winter of my containment as a redhanded thief, though I was in jail, which for some rovers would put a damper on the season as-sociated so long with Old Sock, Old Hat (an undescribed dish of coon and muskydine), and nut-hung trees. Not me. I had everything I thought I needed, with freedom in mind.

I guess I'd sobered up from my fairy-tale ordeal with Amy Survivor, with the shock of the arrest and the cold hard fact of jail. So I lit a match off my burnt thumb, pulled a blanket off the top of a stack, and wrapped it around me. Then, with a sense of luxury, I yanked another one down and half un-folded it on the dirt floor, and sat on it, wrapping it around my legs.

Sitting there in the darkness again I could reach out in three directions, and without getting up have pecans, walnuts, hazels or almonds, crack them in my hands, and eat them, but I wasn't hungry.

That's when something moved under me, by my hip. Cautiously I reached into the woolen warmth of the super-black pitch darkness of that space by my hip and felt around. Nothing was there but space and warmth. I figured maybe it was the shock of being arrested and thrown in jail as a redhanded thief that brought on a cramp in my hip. Thinking thus I dismissed it by breathing deep and sighing, in an old way I had learned long ago, way up the rover's trail, so to speak . . .

Then I felt it again, closer to me now, near my hip, like the ghost of a pistol cylinder revolving in my pocket. I stood up quickly and reached into my pants pocket where the ghost revolved and gently evicted a live mouse risen from the dead . . .

I got into a kneeling position and set the lazarus mouse on the wool blanket, between my knees. A tear rose of its own accord in my dead eye, which sees things inside me and can't hold back.

He stayed balanced on his feet, though I figured he'd roll over, dead again, because how long can miracles last? But he didn't. For a while he just gazed gleaming at the match I'd lit to celebrate and study him, but really, I don't know what he saw before he rolled onto his side, and there was his belly full of acorn bread and shot potential. And for what? Instead of me?

20

The lazarus mouse rolled back and forth between life and death many times that night. I warmed him between my hands set up like a fort around him, till I got tired of holding my arms that way; then I set him between my legs, but ever so gently, to keep him warm and rolling toward light instead of darkness—though I've sometimes known warm darkness. He'd gain his feet, then roll over, his teardrop eyes black as a black stone whose name I can't remember, till finally, when all my matches were used up and my thumb and fore-finger burnt many times over, his black eyes got smaller and dimmed, reminding me of something: hatpins in the hats the ancient roving sisters wore. I was overwhelmed with pity and fatigue, and I stomped on him. The rolling ceased.

I buried him, using Jesus's jackknife, in the dirt floor of the bank cell, in utter darkness. "But not as bad as his ultimate darkness, I guess," I said aloud, just as a winter cricket, probably disturbed by the flashing action of the night and thus not singing, sang as the sun came up way off, and the first pearl light of day rolled under the metal door and lit the outskirts of my blanket.

A knock came to the door and I shouted, "Who is it?" But it wasn't my voice. It was the voice of a thief at home. I folded the knife and put it in my pocket just as the lock unlocked and the door swung open.

There stood that greasy troubadour, Amy's backup no-talent bum, wearing ancient smoked glasses and a broad black hat of straw, grinning like he was somebody. Yellow Hat stood behind him, but was shorter by a foot. The constable spoke as beyond a meaty shroud: "You're sprung."

I didn't jump at the chance like some innocent kid, but in a fairly natural hoarse voice asked Yellow Hat beyond the shroud if he'd do me a favor first: "While I'm still here, will you cash this for me?" and, excusing myself like the polite fool I am, I handed the note around the grinning troubadour, to Yellow Hat, who stood there clean-shaven.

He said, "No. You'll have to come back later, when Billy's here."

"Bill?" I asked, hating to hear a crippled man called by his wrong name.

"Banker Bill," Yellow Hat said. He looked pooped, as if he'd been up drinking and walking through Fate all night.

As they watched I rolled my blankets tight in a single roll stuck under my arm, and stepped out free again, a habit. I figured they'd never miss two blankets, people that rich, and as I was enormously hungry, I wished I'd thieved a handful of hazels.

21

This guy's name, as I found out later, was No Future. Bad feelings about him mounded in me as we walked more or less side by side toward wherever he was going. Honestly, I thought I owed him something for springing me from jail. It was, frankly, a nightmare in there, with the mouse's slow death and all, the onslaught of winter without a moment's notice . . .

After leaving the bank the last thing I noticed was Yellow Hat sucking a bottle of muskydine wine like an old baby before No Future and I turned left where Main Street ended, becoming a road, and walked almost side by side a long way.

Finally, about noon, we made our general destination, a long knobby mesa, with I bet not fifty words passing between us the whole time, things like "uh," "hup," "nuh," and "oops" when one of us would stub a toe on a road rock or turn an ankle in a hole. (Also, I noticed on the trip out of Fate, that No Future's height was partly an apparition, since he wore ancient pointy-toed boots of blue hide that must've been on their hundredth pair of heels; yet, they were in pretty good shape, and, being blue, were suitable for a fancy man, a womanizer troubadour type. In the strong sunshine of noon, I noticed, too, his hat was not actually black, but dirty straw dyed indigo blue.)

I guess I got tired of being an idiot, and just as I saw our destination loom on the horizon I stopped in the terrible road and offered my hand, saying "Mott."

He grinned like nothing had happened bad between us, and it was all bad, and he offered his thin, weak, bony hand to me, saying, "No Future."

That's when I smiled and said, "Blue Hat would be a better name for you."

He stopped grinning and continued walking. The moment of violence in the faded day faded like a fart. That's because he knew I was right, and I shouldn't have said so. The names people take should be more up to them and less talked about.

We walked on, him ahead a little way, and just as we reached a steep rocky path ascending a knob No Future farted for real, turned to me and said, with a smirk, "What happened to the eye?"

"I don't remember. I was just a kid."

Another moment of violence passed. Then I said, "Good thing you're down wind of me, or you'd be eatin' them boots for lunch."

His shoulders bunching, as he thrust himself uphill, showed he heard . . .

But it was stupid talk, as I was reminded when, atop the hill and nearer our destination, I reached in my pocket to check my note, hopefully not crumbling in sweat, and unfolding it in the smell of mouse through the hole, read on the back Jesus's motto: "Between loose talk and silence, opt for silence."

Certainly a wise saying, it is yet hard to apply in real life. Since the last panic, as far as I've heard, it's been traditional in the rover's way to warn a man before you kick his teeth out. But, at least part of my confusion in direction can be explained considering Jesus Green was a treeman, not a rover.

22

With our destination in sight, talking ceased till we got there. Something I've noticed about people is that when they're close to destiny they fall silent, except for necessary sounds of movement and breathing. As a matter of fact, it felt really good not to be arguing with this stranger anymore, for the time being. Then we got within a hundred paces of the place and No Future said, "Ain't you curious as to why or by who you was sprung?"

As a matter of fact I was, but as a matter of necessity I said, "No."

Surely I was falling in with a new bunch of people, not rovers in the true sense, but apprentice musicians about whose ways and wisdom, if any, I knew nothing. However, I did know they couldn't play worth a damn. I wondered who their leader was, guessing they had one, so as a way of relaxing the grip of my threat on No Future (for I tend toward hope by nature), I offered: "Say, you people are apprentice musicians, so who's your leader?"

threshold, just as the woman-haired guy opened the door. I thought, "One step, he's in," in a flashed foreshadowing of events to come.

They went on in, and I stood on the top field stone and looked back at where we'd walked that day from jail. From atop the mesa Fate was fully visible and seen. Somehow, I missed it, the memories; but I was just kidding myself. A rover's life is where he is, and he has to make the best of it. That's also called living off the fat of the land. Same difference. I guess it's true of women, too.

Then somebody put a hand on my shoulder. Not used to being touched, I jumped.

"Take it easy!" said the woman-haired mountain boxer. "Won't you come in?" he said and kind of bowed and swept his hand. His hair fell from his shoulders and smelled of essence; indeed, his voice was not altogether manly. I found out later, in an all-night conversation with him and the guys of the band, that his earnest confusion had led him thus far in life to pick no name: "I pick my mountain box instead," he pronounced in melancholy at dawn following the long night of loose talk.

I've noticed that people will talk loose all night until the sun comes up, suggesting hope and death, and then privately tell some truth, up close to you, like he did, with essence floating from his drunken hair. I may describe that night's talk briefly, later. May not . . .

To skip a lot, I stepped into the house behind the mountain boxer, keeping my eye peeled for Amy. She was nowhere around, that I could see. I already knew she was a lost cause, so I put her out of mind. I figured if I saw her once more it would be in hell or heaven, as I'm not one to judge. Down deep, I try to lead a rover's life.

After initial, useless conversations with No History (the drummer, whose name struck me as perfect, and who was muscular as hell from toting that log, as well as from beating it), and with Head-Dancer, the flute player (so called by Amy Survivor because of his stance and head-dancing technique, though how he could know this I can't say, since she was speechless), I started picking up weird noises from upstairs, muffled gasps, bursting moans, heard through the rotten floors above my head where I stood, more or less in one place, in the big front room—big because empty.

I looked up at the second story floor, wondering. I was about to ask No History what it was, when No Future came slithering down the stairs like a snake in a rotten wall, smiling. Somehow or other he'd eaten good in his life, for his teeth were still in his head, pearly white, what they call "piano teeth," though I've never seen a piano except through a window so long ago, so many doglegs down the trail, that I can't say where, when, or why. So, my unspoken question concerning the explosive gasps coming through the rotten boards upstairs was so much loose talk, water under the bridge, and I let it go unheard.

Naturally, the mountain boxer took me back to the kitchen, where the band kept all their visible provisions: ancient smoky jars of jams; dried squirrel hung on nice hardwood hooks augered to the ceiling; five kegs of acorns; two kegs of almonds; one keg of mixed hazels, walnuts, and pecans big as chicken eggs. There were other things I don't remember. Oh, yes, a line of gallon jugs corked along the wall. At one time there'd been cabinets in the kitchen but they'd been ripped out for some unknown reason, probably to burn, way back when. It was the way of folks, to burn everything they couldn't bury.

Mountain Box stood proudly at the heart of his kitchen, and with sweeping motions showed me their provisions. He was, if nothing more, and still nameless, happy. More than I could show. As far as me calling him Mountain Box, he'll never know and therefore never care, for I never spoke a man's name out loud in my life that he did not take for himself or be given. An exception being that of Blue Hat, on which I gag now, thinking back on the circumstances. Still, by way of self-defense, exceptions in reality are far more worthy of note than a bunch of worthless kitchen talk and moaning around about what I've supposedly, or you've supposedly, never done. Or said . . .

I complimented Mountain Box on his kitchen; he blushed rosy and looked down. That's when I noticed he had no shoes, that his feet had not been washed in ages, and figured it part and parcel of his way of finding his proper name. Also, I figured the Amy Survivor Band were maybe criminals part-time, considering the wealth of provisions they'd amassed.

24

I'll never understand why people take names that don't fit, then live all their lonely lives remaining in daily and nightly trials endeavoring to prove their names do fit. Of course, some folks wise up and bury their old names for new ones, ones they hope fit better or right. But they usually don't.

Names that work are usually ones other folks give us. Given names. Other than that, you're better off without a name.

Not having a name jointly or alone, the band members had gathered in the old house, determined to become one and stronger as a group than alone, a group with a name, The Amy Survivor Band. When the time comes I'll tell you of the success or outcome of that decision.

In my book of wisdom and lexicon I once found a quote that related to my time with No Future, No History, Mountain Box, Head-Dancer, Jesus Green, Amy Survivor, and the others manifesting in and around Fate in those days and nights. It was easy to remember but hard to prove, as it was easier for a deaf mute to argue music than for a toothless gummer to crack a beechnut. Still, a summing up quick in a wise saying, unsigned in a book of such, does not give satisfaction relative to knowing and calmly perusing at your leisure the bare bones of what happened among us, the previously mentioned and me, around Fate in those days. Nothing will.

As I said earlier, I believe certain things happen for no reason at all. For instance, the disappearance of my worldly possessions, except for the clothes on my back, the jackknife and twenty-pecan note with a hole in it in my pocket, and my paper-thin mocs.

And where was Amy Survivor? Gasping in No Future's skinny troubadour's arms? No doubt, I discovered later, relating the painting I stole to the reason I was sprung from jail on a meager one-nut bond.

Even my name would prove vulnerable. As I found out that first night at the clubhouse, that slimy bastard No Future slipped old Yellow Hat an extra nut—an *acorn*, to boot!—to get his hands on my, in turn, stolen name.

25

I found out about it that night as No Future, No History, Head-Dancer, Mountain Box and I sat around the front room on the floor, waiting for Amy Survivor to come down. We had one ancient lantern as light. Mountain Box kept glancing up at the rickety staircase, to where it disappeared in darkness, hangdog like. No Future and No History told their life stories in sickening detail while Head-Dancer cleaned his flute and I fell asleep.

I snapped awake suddenly in the darkness filling the room as No Future, behind No History, Mountain Box and Head-Dancer, climbed the last step into second-story darkness and said, "Night, Mott." The tone of their voices gave the whole thing away; in other words, I put two and two together and got four. In other words, I knew instantly that No Future actually knew my name before I told him what it was back on the trail. You could tell. Don't ask me how you could, but you could. His pearly teeth flashing in lantern light bit off the last piece of Mott.

Also, as the tattered Head-Dancer cleaned his flute on a patch of blue wool scarf he kept folded in his "tux," as he

called it (in a weird word that floats back to me now, recall-
ing how I slept with my dead eye open rather than tell
another made-up story of my life), I heard No Future laugh
about the poverty of Yellow Hat's bribe. And put two and
two together. Also, I found out, later, I was right. Partly. But
you already know I'll never really know . . .

Because I lay there in stolen blankets remembering the
lazarus mouse and the welcome basket (the first of my life)
and Amy Survivor's fairy eyes, the acorns pluck-nuzzled
out of the hills of her bosom, and, in awful still darkness
anyway, sleepy, I unrolled and stepped outside, over the
grassy porch, onto the field stone step, and stood there looking up in dead silence at the same stars that have been there
all my life, and all Jesus's life, and, I bet, before. For some
unknown reason, or from an unknown cause, I chuckled to
imagine all those oak trees dropping their acorns, just for
these outlaws to rob. Bunch of yahoos . . .

I nudged the old porch post with my shoulder lightly, and
thought if I nudged it harder I'd knock the clubhouse down.
I chuckled at that, too, and got caught mid-laughter, a foolish feeling, by a sigh behind me that cut the dead silence
like a voice beckoning your name from the dead, but it was
just a little sigh before your name, a moan cut loose through
the open door of the destination from the rotten dry soul of
the house.

I turned around. Amy stood afloat in a starry gown, her bare
feet pale, her squirrel eyes holes of shadow, on the oaken
threshold. She put out her arms and floated toward me in a
single leap over the vale of grass, a glide so slow it can only
be described in length as equalling a beat of the black heart

of evil perfect love you can't get back. That must have been like it was, though it can't be told. But I'll try.

I received her in my arms, where we locked in her web of hair that smelled (I can still smell it) clean. Her body weight didn't shake me off the field stone. I see now it could have been my headstone, for what I still had to settle for in the field of evil love. Still, there was no evil tea that tasted of tranquility and death that night; instead, her dusky kiss.

If I'd been raised different, in a family I could just piece together now, but not just in the present moment, on the present spot in the trail, I might have handled things differently, better, or had that option. Nowadays, though, I do have brief notions float back in peculiar moments, as for instance when I shave in a mud puddle as geese fly over. I look in my dead eye. I remember dogs and screaming, little and big.

26

Later that night I was lying in Amy's arms, asleep, wrapped in stolen blankets. In a dream I remember I rode the neck of a goose as it flew on the night over Fate. I woke up in a heartbeat, soaked with sweat, in Amy's arms. She looked at me in my eyes as if she was never asleep, and smiled. I want to say her smile was the most beautifully female smile I've ever seen. Yet her eyes were squirrel eyes.

"Weird angel," I said to her, fancy words but not loose talk, and the words just erupted softly from me. I never talked like that in my life. Then she shut her eyes and pulled me up in her arms, having the strength men can't see well in women's arms, and I said, again unwillingly, "I'm thirsty, Amy." And I was. It must have been from the flight. She pressed her mouth softly against mine and filled me with a liquid like honey, salt and water: the precious tears of an angel. I never wanted to pee, but to hold that water within me forever. The bond would flow nourishingly . . .

I fell back asleep. Then I woke up at dawn alone, as I knew I would be, but wishing it wasn't true. A rumbling in the second-story world above me rolled like lonely thunder a hundred miles away that I could still hear, dry in my blankets. Boldly I ascended the stairs into darkness and found a door of wood. I felt it was locked and part of the band's business, and descended back to the big front room where my stolen blankets were, rolled them up and stepped outside.

From the field stone steps I saw Fate misty in the rising sun, gold as an apricot the tinkers sell. Soon it would be white and unbearable.

Suddenly, the house fell terribly silent. By that I knew that the others were asleep, and so took a few side steps and drained my bladder. I hated to. But I had to.

Hungry suddenly, naturally, I stepped back up on the field stones and, fixed to leap back to the threshold, my eye caught sight of a piece of white in the porch grass, which was lush regardless of winter, protected by the roof of the dying porch.

It was a feather.

27

Several days passed in relative obscurity. Everybody went separate directions away from the house, except me. That is, I was the only one who stayed. Each band member took his instrument somewhere off by himself, to practice, I guess. As for Amy, she must have left the house, too, for I didn't see her anywhere, and I searched high and low, going so far as to enter the second story and even rifle the nut barrels, seeking a clue as to the whereabouts of my pack.

Also, I was greatly curious about the criminal nature of the band. I'm sure they had it because nobody in those days had a stash of provisions like that, much less a bunch of no-talent bums learning music from a deaf-mute fairy. Or if she wasn't a fairy, she was a woodland princess, a nut nymph, or just a beautiful woman without mercy . . .

I found no clues to the whereabouts of my pack, but I took full advantage of the cruel aloneness I felt by myself in the clubhouse, not being a member of anything. Rovers make a silent agreement at birth, or before, never to belong. That's their half of the bargain for a free life living off the fat of the land. What's more, I had all the stuff I needed to eat up be-

fore the first real snow buried the nuts for days on end, and
the animals denned up for their long winter's nap, making
the hunting of both about impossible without a rover has a
dog.

Everybody thinks wrongly that the law back in those days
kept rovers from poaching all the pecans and squirrel their
bellies could hold before drifting off to sleep in the warmest
hole they could find to hole up in. Not at all. The snow, especially the first big snow, was the rover's foil.

But—we learned a long time ago how to hole up for the
winter. When everything dies you just bury yourself in it, let
sleep slowly burn the forty squirrels, forty pounds of berries
dried or jammed in bottles tight that you need to eat pa-
tiently but constantly in the few weeks between the first
cold night and the first real snow. You truly fatten up and
waste a lot less by not moving quickly in those weeks. Thus,
guys like the band members—criminals, essentially, poach
or even steal all the stuff they can turn into provisions (for
example, squirrel jerky), then stash it in a safe place far
away from town, finally gorging themselves in the weeks
before the first big snow, then holing up. Fortunately or un-
fortunately, be that as it may, sometimes lazy or stupid
criminal poachers gorge too quickly (without patience) and
not constantly (taking naps) and die fairly young in the
charming stupor that long sleep brings if accompanied by
dreams . . . But that almost never happens to rovers that I
know of, I think due to their natural ingredient of laziness
mixed with good food gleaned—granted, sometimes by others—off the fat of the land.

Looking back on it now, I definitely see how mistaken No
Future, No History, Head-Dancer and Mountain Box were

to gorge themselves in a single week on the forty/forty/forty, in a panic as at night the smell of snow got stronger, and then to foolishly nap now and then without thinking of the future and truly providing for it inside and out. That might sound odd for me to say, considering what I said earlier about the rover's law, but there it is. They were stupid, no-talent apprentice musicians. No. I won't hedge here. The fact is simple: they were simply living on stolen time.

When you consider all those nuts, berries, and squirrels eaten, digested, and growing in people's souls all winter, branching, winding, climbing all winter, changing the plain of the soul into the forest of the soul, it's amazing we don't all fall asleep trapped suddenly in the charming stupor of their dreams, snagged like mice who've eaten too much stolen acorn bread and died like my lazarus mouse, in a stupid charm. An oak tree grew in that greedy fellow, and he just couldn't take it. Who could, when you think about it?

But I happily took the forty/forty/forty provision and, having gone through it so many times okay, I really took my time, fell not asleep, not once, not even in a catnap, and ate constantly the exact amount described by tradition.

But certain things happened that were out of my control. For instance, about a week into my eat, No History came home carrying a huge green sign that he had dug up on the side of the grass-covered highway. He was crying, really beat, as he dragged it over the field stone steps and begged me to help him heft it from the high porch grass (that was still green, though the nights, some nights, had gotten very cold) and up over the threshold.

It was undoubtedly one of the most pitiful displays of man-
hood I had ever seen. I said, as I took one end of the sign
and helped him tote it into the big front room, "You're a hell
of a drummer," but he was crying so hard he couldn't make
sense of it. Or maybe the comment merely fueled whatever
fire had burned him in body and seared him in soul. I'll
never know or even pretend to understand what makes a
drummer tick.

We leaned the sign against the fireplace that hadn't been
used for who knows how many years because it was full of
animal nests, bird nests, one atop another, maybe fifty high,
as one imagines the thickness of a nest inside the height of a
chimney. No History backed off from the big green sign and
just stared at it. Better to say he gazed at it, maybe ten paces
back, then fell like a rag to the floor, dead. I'd seen this kind
of thing before, someplace, and knew there wasn't any use
trying to help him now.

Still, I went to the kitchen fast to brew some tea, thinking,
"I've got to find Amy's tea," though I knew the kitchen, the
whole house, was upside down by then, and knew there was
no tea.

"Just in Amy's pocket," I thought. Then, snapping to, I
raced back to No History, knelt beside him, brushed the hair
from his mouth (for, unlike Mountain Box, he had a mighty
beard uncut for years), and blew my own breath into the
stranger's lungs, one, two, three breaths, till I couldn't take
the smell anymore. You know, the smell of mice. I knew
then where he'd gotten his speed on the drum, his quick-
ness, and the onyx glint in his pebbly eyes.

No matter. I raced back to the kitchen, got some jam of some sort unnamed, and raced back to No History. The jar was well sealed, tight, and I really had to ply my strength to open it: "Who in the hell—?" But I ultimately got it open and put some jam on No History's lips and tongue, then blew into his mouth a bunch more times, applying jam as needed. Not enough to choke him, not even a mouse, just what I needed. No use.

I stood up and looked down at him trapped in his jungly dream. Whatever happened to him on the trail of learning all he could about music had been just too much for him to take. But that's just okay, I figured.

"He's better off going this way than gorging and napping himself into oblivion." I meant the oblivion of vines, branches, berries, nuts, and squirrels looking upon you as a corpse, a nut they keep refusing to eat or bury, till the real snow falls over you like a blanket melting ultimately in the rain of spring, and you dream you haven't rotted a bit and the whole terrible thing rolls around again, the summer, the fall, the trail, never ending and out of control.

I've imagined how it must be; everybody talks . . . I see the hair-roots of a tiny magnolia grasping the hull of an acorn, just holding it, never eating it, because the nut is gone . . . But not No History. His fate was otherwise, whatever fate is. He dug it up and carried it home, to burn it there, he hoped. I bet he hoped that. We'll never know. But we do have a sign, a proof of his intention; for on one side of the sign leaning against the ancient fire hole now housing his histori-cal birds, was the word Fate, white on green, hardly marred by the earth that had hidden it, following the intention of the last panic. On the other side, nothing, just holes where a post had held it up, the name of a town where people still lived.

Clearly, it's tough to bury a fact and just get rid of it. That's what I think I thought when I looked at a drummer, fair at his trade and dedicated to learning, whose last beat was a muffled fall to a rotten floor, now history.

28

I buried No History in a hickory grove near the clubhouse. It wasn't an easy job since the ground was getting cold and it had been raining for several days. I remember thinking how deep the snow would be had it just been cold enough. But it wasn't. Instead, everything was wet, cold, dismally leafless except for little cedars here and there. Also, I had to bury No History fast, before anybody else came home. I wanted to be one up on them, to have something they didn't.

You can see how No History's death had affected me. I was no longer the old Mott. Things were changing inside me, not unlike the weather, due to Amy Survivor. At least, I see now, that was the dream web into which I had flown—or roved. In fact, one of the things about No History's death that didn't bother me much, and helped me dig the shallow grave with a jackknife-sharpened hickory broom handle dating back to the last panic at least, and still hard as a rock, was my feeling that No History had been with Amy Survivor, too, like the rest of her band members.

Of course, I should admit that as I rambled through the house searching for clues to the whereabouts of my pack, I found no evidence of No History, No Future, Head-Dancer, or Mountain Box being with Amy. Still, having become trapped in a dream of my own, I figured my feeling was evidence enough—like that little girl way back in Fate, making her silent father pay his last wages to Jesus Green for a pine tree: because she wanted it, and he probably went without lunch for a week, or her mother went without something, to satisfy the angel's need.

Anyhow, I buried No History in a shallow grave dug with a hickory stick in a grove out back of the clubhouse. It almost hurt to put his naked body in the old cold earth, seeing as how I naturally stole his clothing for immediate and future use; for instance, I wore his coat of leather patches as I dug the grave on my hands and knees. It must have looked odd to the set of crows that hankered around the hickory grove watching me dig—not so much the patch-quilt coattails flying and flapping as I frantically dug, but the fact that I, a man, was even out there digging in the rain and cold, when few people dig, whereas the rain and the cold were the province of the crow searching for dead and still and weak things to eat, constantly searching. Come to think of it they probably hung around cawing back and forth regally in the sleepy hickories, hoping for a peck at No History. I think there were five, but there might have been three.

Anyway, I got the man in the ground and tried to set the sign he toted to his death as his tombstone, but a long, narrow and deep crack could not be dug in the rain-soaked ground; it kept caving in, like a black eye going to sleep, helplessly. So, pissed off, I toted the sign down hill through the hickory grove, where I'd never been or seen, where I came to a fairly deep ravine. It went about fifty feet and lodged against a tree. I don't know what kind.

I started to walk back to the clubhouse, to dry up and continue eating, but something in me said no. I felt dissatisfied, as if a job I'd started was only pretending to be complete. Thus I spent half a day climbing down into and up out of that treacherous ravine, toting that sign, that Fate. I slipped and slid, and by noon, a white dot in the woolly sky, I finally had that sign where it belonged, atop No History's grave, laid flat.

The crows flew away.

29

Back inside I stripped and hung my clothes on the staircase.
I would have hung them on the bannister but it was merely a
fixture of memory, as years before it was burnt for firewood.
So I laid my soaking-wet, ice-cold clothes flat on the stairs;
like a melting man ascending the stairs to the second story,
or descending. I shivered, laughing.

On the floor of the big front room my stolen blankets waited
to warm me dry, and I jumped in, wrapped up tight as I
would on the trail and shivered till warmed sufficient to fall
asleep . . .

I woke up in front-room darkness to the unmistakable sound
of pecans being stomped in the kitchen. Since I knew I
wasn't alone, I lay there a minute to collect my thoughts, lis-
ten close, and decide what to do. I shed the blankets,
figuring to move quieter without them, and walked toward
the kitchen down a crooked hall where at the end I saw the
light of a lantern. Wary, I shivered not. Edging along the
wall I got to the kitchen door and, hearing a nut stomped,
peeked in.

Mountain Box sat with his instrument in his lap, wearing what looked like No Future's hat, gazing at his hands: one on the neck of the thing, the other resting on the strings over the hole. He sat on a chair of wood he must have found somewhere, maybe in a barn.

That was what struck me. Somehow I knew his flight to find music and talent had taken Mountain Box to a barn. The chair was his memento.

He had lit a lantern and sat down in front of it, to play. He looked like he wanted to strike the strings but could not. Frustrated, he took a nut from his pocket, gently put it on the floor under his heel, then with great effort crushed it. The wasted food bled onto the floor, its pity on the heel of his boot.

I shook my head in the outskirts of lamplight. He'd snuck in with his boots on and I hadn't heard. Deciding to let him know I was there, as if he hadn't seen me sleeping, I coughed.

He began to cry, as if he'd just picked up the final clue to his destiny. I saw his tears hit the mountain box as his face fell toward it in the slump of his discoveries. He finally knew what he was, or had found a true and proper name. I knew what it was like to be nabbed.

I dashed back for my blankets, not knowing the nature of his discoveries, and wrapped up tight in them, but not as tight as for sleep, and walked back to the kitchen. I didn't feel foolish, because I knew he was crazy. Nobody in his right mind crushes nuts that way.

When I got to the kitchen I saw that Mountain Box hadn't moved except to sit up, as if to start anew and try to strike the strings. He cried less hard, whimpering like a beggar without talent or a hoax for grub. Detached from his misery, I looked at his indigo hat, surely No Future's hat, and wondered how he got it. Same way he got those boots, I guessed.

To wake him up I yelled, "Play that thing!" but he just could not do it. It was beyond him, then or ever. He looked up at me and opened his lips. Scum stretched between them from being closed so long, and in a fevered burst of gluey tears that rolled over his peach-fuzz cheeks and spattered the use-less box in his lap, he uttered "Ma!" Maybe it's his name, I thought.

That's when I noticed his hair was berry-dyed a different color than it was before. It shone blue in the lantern light, the blue hat atop it. Suddenly he put down his mountain box and started fixing his new hair, fast, like a fancy woman . . .

In no time at all he had it fixed in snake-like twirls spiked out a foot at least from his blue scalp. His hair was thinner than before, too—I figured, from dye and handling. But he seemed satisfied, sighing as he rose from his stolen chair and stepped to the sink. Above it a four-pane window painted by night—like at my shack in Fate—reflected the light. He looked in the window and, awed by ugliness, cov-ered his face with his blue hands, gasped, sucked in air, and raked his eyes bloody with womanly nails, dragging tears and blood to the outskirts of his hair. For a minute he stood real still, framing his bloody grimace in a blur of hands and hair; then he quivered like an infant and crushed the new hairdo, pushed it back from his forehead till I thought he'd rip it out, and smashed it forward onto his blood-burned face, turning it blue as a berry.

It was that purple blue I associate with summer. I guess instead of slowly eating forty pounds of berries jammed in bottles, he'd poured the stuff on his head all at once. Mulberries, maybe. It's hard to understand. I said nothing, and just watched the show, if show it was.

He sat back down on his stolen chair and replaced No Future's hat on his head. Maybe it had rained long and hard on that hat when Mountain Box wore it after killing No Future, and thus dyed his hair that way, I thought. But the hat was just as equally blue and black as it had been before. The same.

Funny how you can hate a guy just by the way he looks. Put on top of that your maiden moaning in the attic, and suddenly you've got reasons. I guess I thought about that for a while, because a moment passed before I looked at Mountain Box again in his chair, holding his instrument. The man looked so pitiful it was hard to explain. The tragedy of his identity and the loss of his hair had done him in. And there's no telling how he got No Future's hat. In fact, I would never know . . .

I guess another man would have comforted him; somehow it never crossed my mind. So I stood there a minute longer in witness of his terror, till he stood up with his mountain box, sighed tenderly, and dragging his chair walked past me wrapped in my stolen blankets, down the dark hallway, up the stairs, and disappeared in darkness, having left the lantern burning strong in the kitchen.

I heard it whisper. I guess in his nightmare Mountain Box could see in the dark as he tramped through a place called home. I'll never know . . . I suddenly had a vision of Mountain Box as a baby dragging his mountain box like a blanket. As it hit his heels and bumps in the trail, it made a song like a lullaby . . .

I smiled to see the kitchen beautifully lit and the big barrels of nuts still there. In my preparation for winter's first big snow I'd barely made a dent in the surface of the hazels and pecans. I'd barely had acorns since they're mostly eaten in the form of bread . . .

Knowing that somehow Amy Survivor was behind all this pain, I searched the closets for jam, to eat some in the quenching of outlandish desire to kill and love. Then it struck me that while I buried No History, Mountain Box must have used all the jammed berries to dye his hair. I looked into the ancient sink (once white) of rust, and, sure enough, berry remnants clogged the throat of the hole. Opening the cabinet under the sink I saw the mass of mulberries, blackberries, dewberries, raspberries, blueberries, and a few dots of wild tiny strawberries, some still whole, wasted there in a pile forty pounds high.

"Amy," I whispered, knowing I'd have to make up the loss some way.

"One thing is sure as hell," I said aloud. "I can't do it tonight." Wrapped up better in my blankets I carried the whispering lantern out of the kitchen, back down the crooked hall, to the base of the staircase. I stood still for a minute or half a minute, thinking to hear more Mountain Box misery, but I heard only the hinting wind in the stuffed chimney puff down, nothing else. I returned to my spot on the big front room floor, and lay down clumsily by necessity, still wrapped tight as a corpse in my stolen blankets, and, like the rover I was, fell asleep . . .

I woke up to a strange boinging sound, *bo-wong*, *wong*, *wong*, like no kind of bird or rodent I'd ever heard. It was pitch dark and I wasn't awake when I heard it. I sat up in my blanket but didn't rub my eyes, for if it was nothing, I didn't want sleep to fall from them. Sleep settles in the dead eye, too, the same amount as in the live eye, in my case, though I've known no other. I guess this comes to mind right now because as I sat there half asleep I heard Jesus say, "Dogbite," but he wasn't even there. Who knows where he was, or what he was hauling? Perhaps he was already holed up for the first big snow . . .

Well, I didn't hear another *bo-wong*, *wong*, *wong*, or anything else, not even winter in the chimney, so I returned all the way to sleep. I dreamed nothing that I can recall, for to do so is dangerous as hell, the oldest trap known to rovers. Due to lack of berries or too much jerky you can dream things that never let go.

I got up in the morning and brewed myself some campfire tea out back of the clubhouse, with some odd grasses I'd found bundled for dry storage in a top cabinet tiny as hell above a hole in the kitchen wall where a square thing used to be. Brittle as leaves in a book of wisdom, it made good tea. After sipping a tiny cup—a cup I'd found in the same cabinet—I looked up at the second story of the rotten club-house, and yelled to stir Mountain Box: "Yo! Ma! Breakfast! Fancy tea!" I'd yelled his real name, I hoped, but no one appeared at any window, broken or whole, around the house. I yelled at them all, not knowing which was his. Maybe his nightmare had snared him forever.

I drank about a gallon of odd grass tea, and toting the cup, barely managed to make it upstairs to find out, finally, what was going on with Mountain Box. Giggling like a silly girl I knocked gently on the door to the second story. When no-body answered I rapped hard on the hollow-core door and shouted, laughing, "Hey! Ma! Play me a ditty!"

Nobody answered and I wasn't gonna wait. I opened the door. As by a thread suspended from a ceiling hook down at the end of the hall, with his old namesake, the mountain box, leaned against the chair below his toes, the dead ap-prentice hung. No Future's boots stood as witness, the blue hat atop them. I found five strings on the mountain box, where there had been six.

I would have kicked that hat into the corner, but dared not touch it for fear the devil troubadour was there, a dwarf in his boots. I leaned the mountain box against the wall by the chair and took the chair downstairs to sit in, pausing at the top of the stairs to look back and make sure I wasn't tricked into a dream. No, it was death for sure: the "Tender." "The Tender," I twittered.

30

My clothes still were not dry, so I took them off the stairs and hung them carefully on the squirrel-jerky hooks in the kitchen ceiling. Loony from the grass tea, I laughed uncontrollably as I hung each piece on a meathook, remembering Mountain Box and his hair, laughing . . . all the effect of the grass tea.

Of course looking back from here I can see how endangered I was under those conditions. For one thing, I had, while burying No History and entertaining Mountain Box, disregarded altogether my eating for winter, and for all I knew, the first real snow was right around the corner (and it was). Also, if Yellow Hat had in his free time, if he had any, gotten too drunk and lost his way in Fate and wandered blind down Main Street, he might have become forlorn and wandered beside himself as far away as the clubhouse. I admit that wasn't very possible, since Yellow Hat was so old and had two jobs back in Fate, but it could have happened, in which case he would have found me naked in the house of the dead, a blue-haired corpse without identity strung up in the attic, the second story.

In any case, and to get both feet solidly back to earth, I'll say that after hanging my clothing on the jerky hooks, I started to hear music, coming from nowhere, in the house. I say coming from nowhere because it was like that: weirdly beautiful but unearthly, unbound by melody, and almost of no tune. I sat on Mountain Box's old stolen barn chair and listened to it with my dead eye open and my live eye shut, the way I listened best in those times, when it hit me where I'd heard that music before: on the dirt street of Fate, and in the pear-shaped, shallow box of No Future's homemade instrument.

Was that where, or was I losing my mind? I don't know now any better than I knew then. Weirdest thing was, I thought it was Amy Survivor plying the strung box to music to snare my drunken soul. Fool I was, it might have been nothing but the wind from an upstairs broken window lamenting through the hole of Mountain Box's sad instrument, less now than it used to be.

I sat there, mesmerized, teased out of action as by the thought, the thought merely, all I had, of Amy's—What? . . . So, in the stolen seat, I went to sleep, another mistake. I was in piss-poor shape, provision-wise, for winter, and getting deeper in the hole . . .

31

Needing a fresh start, I fell asleep, slumped in the chair, to get one. Looking back, I can see my life as a little falling asleep and a little waking up. Since I've purposely avoided all that lies between, as a rover, for the sake of survival, I guess I've missed out on some things, but I feel I made an even trade. After all, I'd seen what dreams did for Mountain Box and No History. There's nothing funny about death in a stupor hung from the ceiling or falling to the floor speechless, wrapped in a web of poaching and fantasy. I'd seen it . . .

I woke with a start, took my clothes off the ceiling and put them on. They were wet and cold and smelled animalish. I knew that twenty-pecan scrip was still in my pocket, but if I tried to look at it, it might tear, being rain-soaked, so I let it go.

Quick as a mouse hearing footsteps on the stairs, I rolled up all the pecans I could, along with the remainder of the dried-grass tea supplies which included a firing device I figured out later how to use, in one stolen blanket from the jail in Fate, and tied it shut with the only thing I could find to do the trick, a braid of my own hair I cut off with Jesus's knife and braided quick to do the job. They used to call that a rover's quirt.

It felt good to be active in the fat of the land. It had crossed my mind, before, to cut a bunch of Mountain Box's dead hair, or to shred his britches for the purpose, but it passed over like a nightmare to somewhere else.

I heard a kicking thump upstairs and ran up there to see what was going on. He hung there perfectly still, but his mountain box had fallen to the floor. If he had swung at all, he swung from a draft in the house. Maybe I could see it move. So he was taken care of. There was nothing left to do but leave.

I slung the sack over my shoulder and, with my other blanket rolled tight under my arm, walked through the kitchen, out the back door of the house, doing so intently to defy the old homesteaders' superstition: to leave through the same door you came in by . . .

About a hundred paces from the house I thought I heard someone call me by the name my mother gave me, which to that moment I had buried under a thousand rugs braided from the hair of dreams I denied the light of day: "Kenji! Kenji!"

I stopped dead in my footsteps and turned like a soldier toward the house. My clothes froze in the sunlight. There, at an unbroken window, on the second story, stood my mother wearing No Future's indigo hat! It had to be! I closed my eyes, to shut sleep from them, for fear I'd die, or was dead and trapped, or I don't know why. On looking again, she waved.

I ran, dropping my sack, to the house, leapt from the field stone, through the front door, up the stairs, through the door, and saw Mountain Box hanging there, still, but his instrument and hat were gone.

"Mamma," I whispered loud, and searched for her through the second story, then, not finding her, yelled her name like a starving child throughout the house. She was not there.

Crying with rage, I guess, I tore off Mountain Box's britches and shirt and stuffed them under the brittle boards of the porch, smashed with my angry feet. Then, remembering, I stripped a few shreds of ancient paper from the walls inside the grass tea cabinet, rolled them in a tinderball and stuck it under the clothing.

I stepped back from the porch and tried to settle down. With senses gathered, staring up at the window where I'd seen the apparition (apparently), I yelled with every ounce of bowels I had: "Mamma!" Nothing. "Mamma!" Nothing. "MAMMA!" No answer.

Shaking, I pulled the ancient firing device from my pocket. Though wet and cold in my pocket, meeting the air it worked perfectly, years not bothering the spark in waiting.

Still, the tinder wouldn't start.

Afraid of wearing it out, wasting the spark, I backed off and thought a minute. I looked up at the window and yelled

"Mamma!" again, remembering a lone pine near No History's grave, and ran to it for needles.

Better than needles I found bone-dry twigs of pine on a dead branch struck by lightning and fallen from the top. I hauled the whole branch back up to the porch and shoved it under the threshold, near where I'd stuffed the tinder wad. Then, in a haze of frantic hope, I struck fire to the pine needles red and dead, which, in turn, fed the bone-dry branch, the wall's paper, the blue-stained britches and the shirt (less the leather belt I stripped from the britches at the last second), and soon the brittle rotten porch boards were ablaze.

I stepped back from the house and gazed at it upstairs. Nothing. Soon, even the oak threshold was eaten by hellfire.

I threw Mountain Box's belt into the blaze, gathered my nuts in my blanket tied shut with my hair, and watched the fire burn the house to the point that the eves caught fire and birds flew from the chimney.

32

Between noon and sundown I covered a lot of ground. I tried not to think about . . . my mom in that window, since before that moment I'd never in memory seen her face. Goes to show that some faces exist before memory or the ability to drag them back. Because that night by the fire I tried to drag it back, her face, but instead all I kept getting was No Future's blue hat. I even went all out, shutting one eye, but nothing worked.

Then I figured it must have been the tea that brought her back, so I brewed some in my hand, using spring water from a precious spring near camp. The tiny bit of old grass and pure cold water worked wonders on my memory, and I could feel something good coming to the surface, but each time it was almost there it turned tail and disappeared, like a bullhead, back to the deep. It was then I wished I hadn't panicked at the clubhouse burn and forgotten the nice teapot of copper I'd also found in the tea closet.

I figured logically I needed more tea, so I brewed a stiffer brew in both hands this time, using a pinch more grass. The spring welcomed my cupped hands as I sunk them in.

Thanks to the strong starlight I could see something buoyed down in the little spring, flowing. I felt it flow on my knuckles, weedy and fine. Very wonderful, I can't tell you what I thought. Alright, I will. I thought of my mother's hair, which wasn't a memory, or of Amy Survivor's hair, which was.

I got to my feet and back to my fire, and drank my tea. I didn't need it. I threw it on the fire, and the fire didn't need it. Two pounds or better of pecans later, fighting sleep, I mistakenly retired to my bedroll and lay there looking at the stars.

Stars neither laugh nor frown, but I get the feeling they're serious. I had that feeling before that night, and later on.

Before I knew it a veil of sleep had been drawn over me. Usually, I felt it pulled up to hand-level first, but not that time. Just as I saw a feist rip the nose off my sister, snow fell fat and heavy on my burning face melting back to life like that bullhead sinking back to the depths of his rightful world, and I sprang awake.

The fire was still going strong. A man sat beside it on a rock, the rock that was there when I made camp and had probably been there many years, the way it looked. The man looked oddly familiar, but I was fairly sure I'd never seen him before. Rangy and stern he wore dark clothing and boots whose wood heels were rounded by the way he sat. He looked at the fire and said softly: "You were dreaming."

I said, "Well, I ain't dreaming now . . . How long you been here?"

He just smiled and poked the fire with a cedar stick that sparked.

"Question be, fella, how long *you* been here?" He spoke softly.

I hated this kind of confrontation, or trail battle, that occurs when real rovers and fake rovers meet. The older man spoke because he knew I wasn't gonna answer.

"Them your nuts?" he said, pointing at the fire.

"What?"

I sprang to my feet and kicked the fire to pieces, as he laughed, jolly as hell.

"I's just funnin' you. Ha, ha, ha. Your pee-cans is over there."

He pointed with the glowing cedar stick to my stolen blanket-sack tied shut with my own braided hair, intact, with hot coals on it now. I leapt over to it powerfully, like a fool, and kicked the coals off it, thereby kicking it untied and scattering probably ten pounds of pecans. Looking stupid, I started feeling around the ground for the nuts and found a few, a handful, when I heard the older man laughing. A bigger fool by the minute I warned, "What are you laughing at?" as if I didn't already know.

Then he looked at me kindly, directly, with a million years of wisdom in his jolly old eyes, somehow young still, and said, "It'll wait till morning. You ain't awake yet, are you?"

I felt on my face. He was right.

Embarrassed, I went over to the spring and washed my head in it, using my hands to cup and rub, but it wasn't working, so I dunked my whole head under the welcoming water, up to my chin. Awake and glad I got off my knees and spun to find the older man gone. In the black, starlit woods I heard no snapping of twigs or tramp of steps on humus ground. Instead, the ghost of heart laughter blew the fire that had entirely, and intact as ever it was, been rebuilt.

33

Good thing the older man came by when he did, wherever he came from, because if he had not I'm sure I would have fallen asleep, really asleep, in the comfort of my stolen blankets, under starlight, with a full stomach. Whenever winter would come with its first big snow I would not have been prepared had I fallen asleep that night—had I dreamed the whole thing.

I sat there on the rock by the fire—an old fire, whose embers might have been going a hundred years by the time I smelled it burning on the trail, a rovers' fire—and figured how lucky I was to have food, clothing, a campsite, and not be dreaming: I still had a shot for spring. If I ate constantly and managed not to doze a while longer I might find a place to hole up in nearby, and I just might survive . . . I had my firing device and jackknife in case I wandered sleepy off the trail . . .

Well, it snowed a whole lot the rest of that night while I walked slowly around the fire, and danced some, to stay gently awake. Not *too* awake, because if you stay *too* awake, oddly, you tend to tire out faster and avoid the new rhythm your body needs for the big sleep, "the long winter's nap," as it has been called forever. Thankfully I cracked duos of pecans in my hands and told dumb jokes to an owl that hooted toward dawn in a great old cedar.

But I suppose the events at the clubhouse, combined with the piece of the dream and the older man scaring hell out of me through the awareness of the fact I had almost fallen asleep, plus the normal fatigue that accompanies trying to form new rhythms, got to be pretty hard, and too close to beyond my control, to be funny. In a last-ditch effort to stay awake I brewed some grass tea for the laughter. Laughter always works. I guess one thing more that made me giggle like a little girl happened then.

Forgetting I didn't have a teapot, I still needed one to brew tea in, so there one was, the twin (practically) of the copper pot from the secret tea cabinet, under my blankets where it would be anyway. I laughed. The older man must have left it, maybe on purpose, maybe not, to say he was sorry for saving my life—a fact which, not being a rover, he may not have understood. But I figured I was wrong. The old man was too quick of wit and fleet of foot, too lighthearted not to know a rover when he saw one.

I looked at the sleeve of my stolen patchwork coat and felt thankful for it, then put the magic pot on my head and danced around in the virgin snow, laughing, spun around and around and fell to the happy ground, already smelling of sleep. Ah, it was wonderful, tempting fate by rolling on its baby blanket! Holding the pot on my head, I rolled like a log down to the spring. I took a big mouthful of virgin snow and spat it out because I couldn't stop laughing, and I hadn't had a drop of tea in hours.

"Maybe the nuts are tainted!" I told the serious owl that watched my every move, and burst into fresh laughter that cramped my gut and brought me to my knees.

The owl flew away and the sound of its wings calmed me down, just as the snow let up and big flakes drifted earthward like hats, them old fancy hats the sisters wore or had hung on trees.

Refreshed from the laughter I took the found pot off my head, wiped it of leaves and hair, and approached the spring but a step away. It was colder than I thought, because the water was frozen at the top, a thin film of ice containing strands of hairy root, probably from the cedar nearby feeding on it year round, I thought. For fun, before breaking the ice, I set the pot on it to see if it would ride. It did. So it was even colder than I'd thought.

"Well, time to go to work," I said to the spring, and kicked the ice, soaking the heel of my moccasin. I slung the smashed fragments to the side and dipped my pot into the tips of root hairs that were nearer the surface than they seemed the night before. Throwing the first potful, I dipped it again, deep, and the hairs, sucked into the sinking pot, swirled finer than other root hairs I'd seen. Lifting the full pot from the spring I carried it up to the fire and placed it on a used forked bois d'arc branch, skinned, yellow and ancient, that I found near the dirt circle around the fire place and propped under a spare sitting rock, thus to dangle the pot above the fire and heat the water without sooting her up.

With the teapot rigged I sat on my rock to warm my hands, which were already warmed by rigging the pot, and to stare at the fire, which I've always enjoyed like company that neither talks nor listens, just stays there, burning, and I began again to fall asleep. Just before I was snapped awake by the pot falling into the fire and damned near drowning out a hundred years of tradition I dreamed or fantasized Amy Survivor combing my cleaned and essenced hair, seated behind me, with me at her feet, in a wild woman's fancy room, looking at me and me looking back in a looking glass of old—of old I know because those things just don't exist anymore. She uttered one sound, "R," smiling, when the pot hit the fire. In dreams the crippled walk and the speechless talk, I hear, though for my part—and I was someone who avoided dreams all he could—I never had two good eyes.

I woke with a start and fanned the fire with my coat, jerking the still-cold teapot from it, and stacked on dead cedar twigs and then branches, fast, to keep it going successfully. Luckily it worked. As punishment I jammed the bois d'arc stick into the fire that it always wanted, being tantalized for years and generations, hung above the fire it wanted but never burning, and thus ended one unimportant, replaceable bit of tradition.

I walked with my pot back to the spring that by now had nearly cleared, and stood above it, watching it clear. One tiny hackberry leaf floated on the marge, and I knelt to pull it out. Kneeling there a moment I recalled the geese of my mud-puddle days and saw that I had certainly aged since my last reflection like this.

"My god, my beard's grown down to my chest," I said, feeling it. "Imagine minnows eating this thing," I said, as I dipped, leaning, the tip of my beard into the spring. Of course there were no minnows there, but the root hairs responded to equals, my whiskers, by whirling near.

Wondering how deep it was, and how fresh deep down, I removed my coat and pulling up my sleeve as far as I could, I sunk the teapot down into the spring, till it stopped. I held it there a minute to let the water clear, and felt the soft root hairs on my arm. Surprisingly, though, I couldn't pull it up; the pot was jammed. I pulled pretty hard, but eased up for fear of breaking the handle, for how would I ever fix a metal handle, ancient and broken?

I figured the pot stuck in mud at the bottom of the spring; it seemed immovable; so I let it go a little and felt that it did not sink. I had muddied the water in the struggle to free the pot, and couldn't see a thing in it, not even the tips of the root hairs.

After entirely removing my shirt (that was finally dry after two or more days of wetness), I lay flat on my stomach by the spring and reached as deep as I could for the pot, found it fairly easily, and pulled harder on the handle. Gradually it rose up, and in it the head of a man, open eyes and all, like a diver surfacing to breathe.

34

Because he kept it tucked under a top hat that suited his tuxedo I hadn't realized how long Head-Dancer's hair was until now, as it hung over the sides of the teapot. As I may have said, Head-Dancer, of all the apprentice musicians, was the most likely to succeed because naturally gifted. I heard tell he played well from the moment he first put flute to lip. Now, here he was, in a teapot. Snared in a happy dream he must have lost his head in the pitch of ecstasy. The longer I looked at his face blue in the virgin snow, the more convinced I became that Head-Dancer had died happy.

Still, I wasn't going to use that spring anymore for washing or drinking. It was muddied for good, maybe for days, for it had not much flow, and I could not see and would not feel what was in it that had made the teapot retrieval so hard. It could not have been the head, for Head-Dancer had been a small man, sprightly as he danced. I looked at the neckflap: ragged and ripped. On one cheek, a small dogbite. This man was beardless. On the other hand, due to his dedication and talent relative to the others, one almost never noticed his face; his flute rhymes were plenty . . .

Well, I had no trouble staying awake. I brewed grass tea from virgin snow. The owl came back.

"Old owl, what do you make of this?" I asked, standing near the head.

He said nothing but turned his head, apparently mystified. It could have been that he was in cahoots with the clubhouse crows, and thus knew more about the Amy Survivor Band and their mischief than I did, having wings, the advantage of height, and a tongue to which I was not privy. According to my combination lexicon/book of wisdom, a bird was an animal with feathers, but I figured they were a whole lot more. Imagine calling Head-Dancer an animal with hair, completely discounting his music . . .

The tea was good. I was catching on fast to its powers, and used just enough to produce warmth, but not mirth, in the magic teapot full of hot, shrunken virgin snow.

While Head-Dancer watched me on the verge of laughter, a mockingbird flew from the cedar to this head and touted a riddling tune whose root lay in the breast of some other bird. One up on the mocker, dead happy, his silent ditty still original, Head-Dancer blew a bubble from somewhere. It froze on his lips, shining, and before it burst, if it did, I had packed, picked a direction, and prayed never to see Amy Survivor again, especially in a dream.

35

The snow fell harder as I ascended and descended a series of hills away from Head-Dancer Camp, and in heavy snow arrived at a woodlet of black oak. On leaving camp I'd determined never to look back on the house where Mountain Box (so-called) had hung himself or the camp where Head-Dancer had lost his head. Horror and death were very bad dreams of which I wanted no part. The same was true then.

So you can imagine how glad I was to find the little black oak forest floor covered in about a foot of acorns, but the snow was wet and falling fast, so I had to gather as many as fast as I could. For all I knew, it was the first real snow of winter, but it wasn't . . .

As the trail away from Fate disappeared in the shroud of snow being woven to live around me, I gathered maybe five pounds of good acorns, eating none raw, till the pockets of my borrowed patchwork coat were chock full. Make that my stolen patchwork coat, if it is possible to really steal from the dead . . . I guess it isn't . . .

Not knowing if it was noon or later, I determined to camp in the woodlet, as it was high on a hill. In luck, I found a giant cedar atop a rock all by itself in the heart of the woodlet, and set up camp at its base. On ground essentially dry I opted not to have a fire, just sat in my blankets from the jail in Fate, and ate pecans, maybe a pound cracked by hand, figuring to bake and eat the acorns later on, further down the rover's trail. I'd form them in hat loafs and bake them black, the way I liked them, when the opportunity presented itself.

"Maybe in the next town," I said to a pitiful squirrel oddly thin within this treasure trove of acorns. I tossed him an acorn, which he rejected. I guessed few rovers used that trail or ever camped under that majestic cedar, since the squirrel just stared at me after I beaned him by mistake with the hatted acorn. I wondered, frightened, if I'd knocked him out, another death. But no. I tossed him a fat pecan and he buried it immediately. Then he scampered off.

Glad to see him go, because I wanted to be alone, I popped a perfect half pecan in my mouth and decided to rest my eyes for a minute, or less. There was a trick rovers knew for resting their eyes and not falling asleep. It was to stare at nothing. But the snow knew a better trick. As it fell on a man wrapped in blankets and dry, the snow hummed a lullaby. That lullaby was too real for words. It was so sweet you could open your mouth toward heaven and eat it. In so doing you could see cold nourishment falling from oblivion, too much to take, but not all there is. Sleep came next, and its handmaiden, Dreaming . . .

With her I woke up in my blankets under the cedar. It was dark. I was glad to be alive. The snow had stopped. A rabbit hopped carefully past my head wrapped in the blankets and paused where the snow started at the outer edge of the clear ground under the cedar. He sat there frozen, his cottontail to me. At dream speed a dog leaped over my head and snared the rabbit, which died instantly. The rabbit was better than dead. He wasn't dreaming . . .

I woke up again to the smell of dog. I've always known the smell of dog. It's like the smell of mouse, but bigger, rougher. It is like a hundred times the smell of rabbit. The snow had stopped. I didn't move. Up through the cedar I could see a big winter star in the cold oblivion. I judged by smell the dog was close, but only one. Instinctively my knife lay open under my hand on my chest, over my coat, under the second blanket. I knew the dog knew I was awake because no matter how long a rover roves, a dog knows better. It roves further. I've seen pups who rove in their sleep for sale in baskets in town like Fate, from ocean to ocean. I've seen dreaming pups rove and kick and roll their eyes asleep as creeps like No Future toss them into boiling pots.

With that in mind as a trick to control my smell, sympathize it, I turned my head to the dog that lay asleep at the place where your eyes have turned as far as they can in your turning head without getting to your feet or rolling your body. The rangy hound lay bloody and blond, dying in the starlight under the cedar, with me. Steam rose from its guts laid out within my grasp, had I been hungry enough.

Sure of no threat, I whispered "Boy," but got no answer. I whispered "Boy" louder, but the dog didn't move. I figured he was near death and I owed him something, for his smell had woken me up. I could have been dead asleep, if not for this dying dog.

"Boy," I said aloud.

He lifted his head and looked at me for the last time, but I knew this dog had seen me a hundred thousand times. That was the look in his dying eye. He poked his tongue out, as dogs do, under their noses, and sighed as dogs do, though their noses, and his gut gurgled, and he died with starlight in his eye. It was cold. He'd last till morning.

"Squirrels don't eat dog," I thought . . .

I woke up some time later, in dark snowfall. The dog was gone. I reached out of my blankets and swept over the dry ground, seeking the dog that might as well never have died there, because he was gone.

"Crazy world," I thought, tucking my arm back in. "Crazy world of maybes."

Then a dog howled on the hill. I shut my eyes again, tired of waking up to dreams, and fell asleep, sweet, sweet sleep without dreams. It's sweeter than the honey of love, because honey contains the bees of dreaming, a hard lesson I learned when I got stung by love unborn, before it even hatched from its cell in the hive of dreams hung in the hollow of the tree of dreams not tremendously too far a walk from the black oak woodlet where I finally fell asleep to the howling of a puppy for its mother.

36

Please try to grasp the fact I woke up to the mixture of a real dog howling on the hill and a dream dog licking my face. Otherwise you won't know what happened as I reached for her, the handmaiden, and she wasn't there. Instead I had a foot of new snow like a wall fortifying the clearing under the cedar. You might imagine how startled I was, fearing this was the first real snow of winter and the fact that I wasn't sleepy in the face of it, but wide awake and rested.

"Jesus," I thought, wishing he were there to dispense the wisdom of his years. But he wasn't.

Traditionally I put a pecan under the cedar for the haggard squirrel, then took a piss and packed up tight to hit the trail that wasn't even there.

This is what you would have seen from the hill above the woodlet: a huge cedar surrounded by oaks, a little squirrel crossing the snow to the cedar, and a redhaired rover stepping out from under the tree. The little squirrel replaced me under the tree as I tramped up the hill.

With snow in my moccasins and the remainder of my nuts

mixed in my hair-tied blanket-sack thrown over my shoulder, I knew I had to find a place to hole up for my long winter's nap, and find it fast, for it could be winter's first real snow had already fallen. Certainly my provisions were low and my forty/forty/forty plan shot to hell.

"Where will I find forty pounds of squirrel jerky in this wilderness?" I wondered as I climbed, "let alone forty pounds of berries jammed in bottles?"

Then, just as I crested the hill I smelled smoke. Invisible, it smelled of dog nonetheless. Excited in my lungs for the crest I slipped and fell flat on my face in the virgin snow, but scrambled to my feet, barely losing a second of valuable time. I cursed the hill and the handmaiden of sleep, but loose talk gets you nowhere. So I opted for silence of thought, and got to the top of the hill.

It paid off. Maybe a hundred yards away, tucked in a vale, with jerky strung on wire beside it, stood a conestoga I'd seen somewhere before. Smoke in a thin ribbon rose into stillness beyond it. I breathed deep to smell the dog, and hungrily descended toward the wagon in the vale.

As I neared the wagon I noticed lots of dog tracks in the snow and yellow suggestions of a pack of maybe twenty dogs, large and small, encircling the vale. I guessed a road passed through there, if you could see it. (That was part of the trick of the snow: the equalling out of things asleep beneath it.)

I stopped short of entering the wagon camp, and peered through a nice stand of post oaks first. Couldn't see much, other than the racks of jerky that made my mouth water with need, and at my feet the snow riddled with dog tracks.

"I wonder what happened here," I whispered. I yelled, "Yo! Hello there!" but, as usual, got no answer. "Yo! Hello! Anybody home?" I yelled, and got no answer.

Sunlight-melted snow dropped from an oak to my shoulder, or was shaken off. I looked up, and saw nothing, figuring a crow. Naturally I yelled out loudly one more time: "Hello! Anybody home?" but got no response.

So I stepped gingerly through the oaks to the jerky rack, sorely tempted to pull one down to chaw, but I refrained. Instead I breathed deep the strong smell of roasting dog that came from the fire beyond the conestoga. Judging by the jerky and the sizable wagon I figured the family that lived in it was wealthy.

"Must be," I whispered as I rounded the wagon, my hand on the rich wood, the ancient wheel. The raw wheel was road-hardened. I wondered how it was made, by what hand, in what ancient tradition old as the hills without names, and counted the spokes. Sixteen. The grease on the axle oozed black and sappy. I fingered a scoop of it for my forehead, cheeks, and lips, which were hardening from the cold.

Rubbing this on, I stepped across the wagon tongue and saw the family scattered hither and yon, their sexless bones asleep at last on the blood-spattered snow. There must have been a lot more than twenty dogs, for I counted twelve skulls. The family consisted of one big man, his tiny wife, and their ten children, the youngest an infant. I knew the wife from the others because her ring was still on her fingerbone. There wasn't a shred of meat left on any of them.

At the center of the tragedy the fire burned merrily under a big dog on a spit. Oddly, the father's hat hung on the spit. I took it off and wore it because I needed one and it fit my head perfectly. I took it off and looked inside it, as one does with hats that are new. A long red hair, the color and thickness of mine, nested deep in the crown. A memory of my father flooded my eyes, faceless but with eyes, and his tongue ripped out, and it had to be true, truth being the father of memory, whoever the memory is. Nothing floods the eyes like truth, and for a moment I felt my dead eye see, as through the truth-crack the dog had ripped in it.

But it was only the veil of tears through which I saw the ribbon of fire-smoke collect at the heart-hole of the roasting dog, then rise thin and undisturbed, for there was no air. No air! Replacing the air, the smell of dogmeat smoked perfect and the freshet of blood and snowmelt at my feet, flooding my moccasins as the strong sun rose to noon.

"Enough's enough," I commanded myself.

I set to work gathering all their bones as one family again, and heaped them on the hungry fire, after eating the dog's heart in their honor. A large calico bonnet, probably the wife's, lay in the shade under the wagon. I fetched it for a head rag to wear under my hat, especially fit for an ear cover. It was of padded wool, a winter bonnet she must have been proud to wear. I would wear it with pride, in her honor especially, whoever she was who heroically bore ten children into this trying world.

37

At least I saved their bone marrow from the dogs of hell who would come back when their bellies were empty . . .

It clouded up again, and snow fell, turning to rain, but I kept the fire roaring hard and high by piling on dead oak and bone-dry cedar branches I found stacked like skeletons under an old fallen cedar up the dirt road that appeared as the snow melted in rain.

As the snow melted in gentle rainfall really like mist, children's clothing appeared all around the site. Boots, a bonnet, a hat. Pants and dresses the dogs had ripped to shreds in their pillage of the family. I figured the people were gatherers working the nut harvest when their wagon got stuck in the mud two days east of Fate. Tough luck. But they bravely built a homey fire, a brave one to boot, and, hungry for meat, ate a wounded dog that hankered into camp. It might have been the wounded animal that led the hunting pack there with his blood on the snow. The bigger kids might have been playing house in the fallen cedar up the dirt road, as up there I found the boy's hat (like his dad's, but smaller, homemade) and a big rag doll.

As the sun fell I searched up the road for signs of life, maybe a child in a tree. I found nothing, but was hopeful for a minute when I heard squealing in a hackberry thicket. On penetrating it I found a rabbit trapped in a hole under a tree.

"Now, how did this happen?" I said as I reached for the cottontail and pulled it free. It felt good to touch a living thing with a beating heart again. The rabbit ran away with the experience. I took it with me, too . . .

God knows how they afforded such, but I found blue ribbons, still tied in bows, in the road a little farther up. My thumbs fit through the ribbonholes. The rain increased. I looked down the mud road at the pyre still raging, raging in the rain that couldn't kill it. The family's souls were burning too hot to drown in tears that came too late, though that's the way with tears, even heaven's. They come too late. Could be the tears of heaven served to fuel the fire . . .

I climbed up into the wagon and found maybe fifty pounds of pecans in sacks marked "Good-As-Scrip!"—a rare brand. Moreover, I found twenty bottles of blue grape jam that had to have come from way up north, leading me to think the family were adventurers aiming to nest south of there somewhere and working the nut harvest for payment in kind as they went. I marveled with pity at the assortment of iron tool heads and blank hickory handles stacked under blankets in the bed of the conestoga: proof they were nesters, or aiming to be . . .

The night turned cold, and rain to snow, as I hung back in the conestoga and ate as much as I could of the blue jam, poked my head out the front every once in a while to check the fire crackling in the snowfall, and thought about, of all things, women, and not naked sex women, but women in calico, wearing smiles of good teeth like I never had seen, jamming grapes. I smiled, beside myself, just to think of them. Then, naturally, my mind turned to naked women I'd never seen before, either.

I started getting drowsy and took a gander at the fire. Out around it, standing in snow, stood the Conestogas, Father in hat, Mother in bonnet, and stairstep kids in an unbroken circle, staring at the fire that I was staring at, too. I scooped snow off the wagon seat, and rubbed it on my dead-tired face, to wake up. When I opened my eyes, they were still there, holding hands. I couldn't take it. I felt bad, wearing her bonnet, and her out there bareheaded. I wished I had Head-Dancer's flute so as to entertain them with a death-song, but I couldn't have played it, anyway.

The wheel grease melted on my stone-cold face as I must have been fevering. I lay down in the tool coverings, and shut my eyes that burned with dream fever. I'd eaten their provisions, stolen their clothes, and commandeered their wagon. Maybe they needed it all back.

"Who knows what the dead need? Who knows what the *dead* need? What's a rover know, a one-eyed rover with a name stolen from a dead boy's love letter? Jesus!" I pled in the wagoneering night as the first real snow of winter fell in flakes like tiny hats off the heads of frozen angels . . .

Shaking so hard I couldn't hold the blankets closed over my chest, I woke to an eerie music strung through the hum of the snow that now had fallen so heavy that the tarp sagged

117

somewhat under it. I recognized the tune. I'd heard it played by an angel somewhere, some time hazy and lost.

I sat up in my stolen blankets, the quilted tool covers, and listened. Fearful and fateful, I rolled out of the covers and peeked out the front of the wagon. The family walked up the snowy road, in the direction of the fallen cedar that still fed their fire. The farther they progressed, the dimmer their fire. And the farther they progressed, the dimmer their music. Ultimately they crested the next hill, glowing like foxfire as they did. And the music vanished as the snow fell hard again, having let up some for their ascent of the hill.

To preserve my energy I let the fire die, and returned to my tool covers. As I rolled them up tight I noticed my fear was gone, and felt lucky and grateful for the ghosts' generosity, glad they were together still, taken by an angel to a nest in heaven.

38

The sun rose on two feet of new snow. Still, the pilgrim fire smoked. Had I wanted to, I could have hung a pot of virgin snow from the spit hook and had me some tea, but I was already so full of blue grape jam and "Good-As-Scrip!" pecans that a mouthful of mirth tea would have made me puke or cramped me up, so I refrained.

I set the remaining bottles of jam, the rest of the pecans, and all the squirrel jerky in a handsome pack that must have been the father's from the old days (I thought with hope how he might have been a rover), tied my bedroll of two blankets to the top of the pack, and hefted it onto my shoulders. They welcomed the weight, and I sighed, stooped in the wagon, to think of the timepiece I took to be my father's (which was highly unlikely) either belonging now to some thieving troubadour, or still in my pack back in the Nut House in Fate . . .

By noon I'd put lots of tracks in the virgin snow between me and Rag Doll Pass—what I called the site where the family of twelve pilgrims were eaten by dogs, and whose tragic demise enriched me physically through the provision of squirrel jerky, blue grape jam and "Good-As-Scrip!" pecans that by hook or crook would not have lasted the pilgrims a winter, but might have gotten them to the hard road to Fate, where somebody like Jesus Green could have saved them. Also, they enriched this rover spiritually in the witness of their unity even after death. I knew that, with luck, I had a chance to go to heaven, too.

Another fact leading me to call the site Rag Doll Pass was the miracle of the little girl's rag doll ascending into heaven behind the guardian angel, with the others whose footprints were buried under two new feet of snow . . .

I wonder, now, how I must have looked to the five crows hankering for dots of flesh in the blood-buried snows of yesterday mostly melted in the rain, turned to ice under the two new feet of virgin snow, as I plowed with feet in stolen leggings the house of snow and icicles under the fallen cedar whose limbs had cremated the family's bones to spite the dogs, had burned in the fire of their pilgrim souls, as I searched and searched for that doll. But the doll was gone to heaven, too, which I took as proof that dolls have souls.

"Of what use to a dog is a doll?" I thought, as I crested the hill above Rag Doll Pass, and saw before me, stretched out as far as the eye could see, the outline of a massive two-piece highway buried under snow. And there was no better trail than them grass-covered highways, especially when you were navigating across unknown territory buried under the first two feet of the first real snow of winter.

"Good news," I said earnestly, aloud, as I re-hefted my stolen pack full of stuff and pulled the hat-bonnet combination down tighter on my head, and set off tramping without a single thought of where I'd hole up for my long winter's nap, or how, hearing the crows caw behind me for blood, their jerky.

39

"Damn it, Mott, your feet's half froze! Shoot, boy, you might be dead by sundown!"—I was cussing myself to keep a constant tramp down that miracle road buried under two feet of new virgin snow, knowing there would be more by dusk: the twilight when any sensible rover was holed up, edging into his long winter's nap . . .

"But, no, not you, fool . . . Got to meet up with a bunch of no-talent bum musicians and lose your head to a deaf and dumb fairy Nut House waitress!"

I kept having to yell at my feet in the oblivion of endless road, blind ramp of snow without a soul on it but me, because they more and more felt frozen; and as I looked both left and right (and, even more foolishly, behind me, to see the snow-blind realm I'd already passed), I saw nothing suitable, by the furthest stretch of the imagination, for holing up.

Once I had to stop in the center of that great ramp of snow, to stomp my feet on each other, to liven them, but I couldn't feel a thing in them, or through them. Without a place to go, I was a goner. .

For some reason I looked up at the sky, the sparkling blue firmament, and closed my eyes, both of them. There I stood in my stolen wardrobe, wrapped in sunlight, tired as hell, freezing and scared, with my dead eye shut: a bad sign.

Then I smelled horse to the north, whence the wind bore down toting its next bag of virgin snow. I smiled to smell horse, and without opening my eyes I lifted my arms to the firmament and shouted "Ho!" That's when he snorted and ran off. But I was not disheartened much. Still happy-wild to be a rover, I knew the horse would come to jam, so I opened a bottle and ran on stubby feet to get upwind of him. Though I hadn't seen him yet, his tracks wouldn't lie, couldn't.

I found the white animal a few minutes later, nuzzling a mound of snow on the eternal plain of the same. A lead rope hung from his halter to the snow. I held the blue grape jam out to him; he smelled it, wild-eyed. I noticed fresh scabs hardening on his belly and neck, where dogs had tried to take him down.

I felt proud to have this horse as mine, even before he was. A fairly tame animal, he ate the jam from my hand (which, licked clean, I quickly stuck in my coat pocket), but ignored the rest I dumped on the snow, instead returning to nuzzle the hump of snow. He snorted in the hump, and pawed it slightly. He looked at me and whinnied.

I brushed the virgin snow from the mound and found my horse's twin buried there, eyeless. Eyeless in the socket that looked up, cleaned out. On his head were a lead rope and halter just like his brother's. I wiped more snow to find most of the shoulder gone, the ribs bare of meat, the bloody virgin crystals of snow.

I put two and two together and realized what I had here: a team. With but two horses, even a good match pair like these, it was no wonder the pilgrims got mud-stuck in Rag Doll Pass. In rain, the dogs came, a horde from hell, large and small; then rain turned to snow, burying the tragedy, which is what I did, to defy the crows, when I scooped arm-fuls of virgin snow and dropped them on the dead horse. When it would snow again that night—and the sky was al-ready turning gray—the horse's mound would look nothing like a horse, but twice that size, and the blood smell would be buried for a little while.

I looked at the live horse. He looked humble. Might be he was sad.

No crows lurked within sight. I swung up onto the white horse like I'd been his forever, and he walked off slow but stout, the past buried till spring, toward wherever we'd be that night.

40

I must have fallen fast asleep on horseback, or passed out from pain and exhaustion—maybe both—because I woke up with a crash, still aboard White Horse, as the poor critter collapsed, dead as a doornail, on the straw-covered dirt floor of a stable attached to a much-heard-of infamous house of pleasure prophetically called The Beautiful Woman Without Mercy, in the legendary ghost town not to be found on any map I've ever seen, The Town With No Name. I guess it was dusk of the same day I left Rag Doll Pass, but I can't say for sure, for when you fall fast asleep on a moving thing you hardly know how much time has passed . . .

Odd, and pretty telling it was, too, how, like the rest of the poor souls I'd met since I camped out under that lightning-struck pine east of Fate, and caught that ride with Jesus Green, and met Amy Survivor and her crew of no-talent bum musicians (not really, not all of them), White Horse also fell eternally asleep in the grip of a dream. For there it was, a wooden manger, or hayrack, if you will, full of sweet alfalfa hay from who knows where, one step away, a neck's length out of reach . . .

I hoped his soul got there, or farther, after all he'd been through, after all he'd done for me . . .

As it was dusk I had daylight left, and decided to explore The Town With No Name. Luckily, when I decided to walk away from the carcass of the animal that saved me, my feet still worked. In fact, I could feel my toes. I knew, though, that snow would fall again when night fell.

I wondered if I'd see any ghosts in The Town With No Name, especially the ghosts of wild women. I'll swan, though, the place was as near a replica of Fate as a ghost town could get, considering it was a lot older than Fate and had no living residents of flesh and bone to keep it up.

The nut house had a colorful name, The Horn Of Plenty. Its sign, shadowed under a brow of virgin snow, said "The Horn Of Plenty" over a huge horn which must have been from some foreign land, full of fake nuts carved from rock. The horn itself was bolted to the wall of the nut house, but since the rock nuts were just laid in there loose, I wondered why rovers and others passing through hadn't stolen individual fake nuts for souvenirs of their stay in The Town With No Name. It was one more thing I might never know.

As would be expected, there was no glass left in any window of the local nut house, or in any other window in The Town With No Name, as surveyed by me from Main Street in the waning minutes of dusk on the second evening of the first real snow of winter in those days. I must add, too, I reveled in loneliness as I searched through town for what I could find, for I had plenty of provisions, good clothing, and the hope I might still make the rhythm right for a safe, long winter's nap, before the snow got too deep to traverse.

I looked in glassless windows, through panes of air, from the covered sidewalk that ran up and down Main Street, as you might recall was true also of Fate. Here, the roof over the walk was gradually collapsing under winter after winter of snow, and in places I had to walk in the street because I couldn't pass beneath it without crawling through rat-infested roof-wreckage, which I wasn't about to do, of course . . .

I felt in my britches for Jesus's twenty-pecan note, which I still had. I found it, and poked my finger through the jack-knife slit cut in it. It felt good to have that money, though I had no doubt the bank in The Town With No Name was closed forever. Also, I had plenty of pecans from the conestoga back in Rag Doll Pass, enough to last me all winter, if I slept right, all or most all the way through.

"I'll spend just as good next spring," I said confidently out loud, as I about-faced and headed, with nut-jam-jerky energies aplenty in reserve, back toward The Beautiful Woman Without Mercy house of pleasure at the other end of Main Street. Though I had as yet seen no ghosts, I did not feel unwelcome voyaging among their houses, not discounting as unwarranted the occasional wail.

41

Snow and night fell one by one as I neared The Beautiful Woman Without Mercy house of pleasure, and saw White Horse lying under the manger at the far end of Main Street, all the collective light of snowflakes illuminating his dead blue eye. I remembered his brother buried under a hill of snow as, in the final magic of nightfall come on down, I rapped bareknuckled on the massive front door of the whorehouse.

From what I'd heard, up and down the trail of life where I'd changed my name a thousand times, or a hundred, I judged that was what a house of pleasure really was.

Of course, nobody answered. That was more or less this whole story, in a way. Still, to be polite, even among the ghosts of whores, I knocked a few more times. Nobody answered. Then I thought of a substitute, crazy trail fantasy. I figured I could strip the stable of ancient lumber, build me a bonfire, fix up a grill of whorehouse curtain rods, and barbecue my horse a piece at a time over the next few days, till I was ready to hibernate. It was, like I say, just a substitute fantasy I supposed I needed in place of a whore, till the massive front door of The Beautiful Woman Without Mercy opened, apparently of its own accord, and I stepped in . . .

The place was pretty dark, as night had fallen, so I felt along the wall by the door like a blind man in a haunted house, looking for a source of light. I found a candle, but couldn't light it with my fire starter. Needing tinder I ripped off a piece of ancient curtain, frayed it with my knife, and lit it, then lit my candle off that. I dropped the curtain piece burning to the floor, and stomped on it to put out the fire, for fear of burning down the whole whorehouse. The cloth burned most dirtily. I had a hard time putting it out, and thought I heard whores' laughter in the room (which, by the way, was quite large for a parlor in a house of pleasure in such a community).

I yelled, "Shut up!" just for fun, now that I had light, then proceeded to explore the whorehouse.

I found a few interesting things that had apparently been overlooked by previous rovers, passers-through, and what-not, who, I guessed, hunted souvenirs, as I was doing. To an extent, though, I wasn't looking for something to keep, like some dreamer, but just looking. I feel you know what I mean. When a rover passes through a house of pleasure he ain't looking for something to keep. He knows the pleasure ends. If he's lucky there won't be any unpleasant reminders, which is sometimes the case among rovers who hang around houses of pleasure, seeking souvenirs. They're usually young and don't last the winter.

Anyway, I found a clutter of items in a kitchen closet,

things dating back to when The Beautiful Woman Without Mercy was a going jenny. I guess you could loosely call these items tools. Since they're good for nothing nowadays, I'll not describe them. For instance, what good is a velvet whip?

Taking it in my hand a picture of the Conestoga Family naturally arose in my mind. Father, whose hat I wore as I stood there holding the velvet whip, walked alongside the pale horses struggling through the virgin snow, encouraging the twin blue-eyed steeds, stout and ignorant of the future night when, around the happy campfire, he and his panic-stricken family would make a hearty meal (that simple) for the roving dog-horde of hell. I further saw his wife, driving the feeble team from the high seat, beating the horses with a real whip of leather, horn in the handle; her offspring and his crowded into the picture in my mind, huddled around her, jostled in the wagon, laughing as the first real snow of winter, death's virgin, behatted their eyelashes, hats, and wagon tarp stretched on warped bois d'arc ribs rattling toward the town called Fate that they would never reach.

I tossed the velvet whip into the same closet where I'd found it, figuring afterward how the rovers and whatnot, before me, passing through The Beautiful Woman Without Mercy, surely had done the same. Then I shut the door and locked it with an ancient silver key that was in the lock when I'd found the closet locked in candlelight. Then I wondered with a certain sense of consternation why nobody had stolen that key as a souvenir before, always returning it, ultimately, to its hole.

"None of my business," I whispered, shielding my candle's

flame with my free hand, and headed upstairs to face the ghosts of whores.

"Better than a dead horse in the barn," I joked for warmth, figuring I'd bed down out there, if not for my long winter's nap, then just to rest my eye a spell.

42

Upstairs I went room to room with my candle but found no ghosts and not much left by the ravages of time. A few old pictures scattered across the floor of one room excited some interest. At one time colored, they now possessed but the ghost of color. They were of absolutely naked women doing various things of little or no importance with each other. Still, they appeared to be having a good time.

In one picture, the best of the bunch I saw, a woman seemed on the verge or even in the midst of being trapped by a dream, and I figured if she died that way, at that fevered pitch, with her eyes shut, it would be hard for her to take an eternity of such a dream. It was just a picture of her face.

I sighed a deep sigh of relief to have found, if not a real ghost of a woman of pleasure, at least a picture of one, and in my mind knew I was better off with the picture as a souvenir of my stay at The Beautiful Woman Without Mercy than I would have been with the whore's ghost herself.

"What is a man going to do with a whore's ghost, anyway?" I reasoned as I walked with my candle to the end of the hallway upstairs. I wanted to look out the intact window at the end of the hall. As I approached it I remembered Mountain Box strung up in the clubhouse, and then imagined him burning. Nightmarishly, in my imagination the blue hat didn't burn. The clubhouse burnt to the ground, but No Future's indigo hat was taken back to him by the crows of death . . .

I stood with my candle at the window and looked at the vast plain stretching out forever under gently falling virgin snow. Then I did a somewhat brave thing for a rover alone in a haunted house of pleasure famous for its ghost whores I hadn't met. Risking direct contact with the dead, I blew out my candle, to better see the virgin snow blanketing the land of the living and the dreaming, the plain old live and dead.

43

I stood there a minute in reverence for how things are and suddenly realized I hadn't eaten in hours. "This could be the end of me," I thought as I felt my way along the wall toward the staircase leading down and out of the whorehouse, a blind man again, when something, maybe a fixture, snagged my stolen pack.

In a panic I pulled free and spun around to face whatever it was.

Between me and the window where I'd stood revering reality bobbed black silhouettes of mad figures in pursuit of rover's meat.

I tried to escape along the wall, but the hungry ghosts of whores and rovers and whatnot trapped in The Beautiful Woman Without Mercy packed the wailing hall so tight that all I could do was hold my own in the soft web of their destiny. I did so by shutting my eyes and thinking of something else.

I felt a velvet whip dragged across my cheek, cold and evil

as a snake. Soft fingers made of whispers pressed my lips as others made of muscle pressed my crotch. I rolled against the wall, but the wall rolled away, and even with my eyes shut I could see the color red. I didn't open my eyes, though I felt a woman's ribs in my hands and her bust against my chest. I gasped as her whispery fingers clung to the back of my neck like cold webs fallen from an ancient loom. My clothing fell away like bark stripped by lightning, but my limbs and core thrilled to the harm.

The bare whore was on me, a beautiful spider pressed belly to belly with her foolish prey. But like a bee rolled in a silken web, I had one stinger, and stung her to death, but a moment's death, for as I felt her release, her cold mouth fell afire to my gasping mouth and flooded me with honey melting to salt water on which I gorged and gagged. I felt my heart dislodge and churn for the sea of love in time churned by the ghostly hips of her rose lips locked in mine, squandered on a candy souvenir that melted in first light as I opened my eyes on a calico maid drifting down the whorehouse hall.

I sat there a long time in bitter regret, till I hung my head remorsefully, and my stolen bonnet's padded rim entered my field of vision, and I saw that its homespun matched the ghost whore's homespun. Or perhaps she was merely the ghost of a housekeeper in The Beautiful Woman Without Mercy.

I pursued her through the house, yelling "Amy! Amy! Amy!" like a madman, which I guess I was. I had not seen her face, and her hair was knotted on her head, tight as a ball, so its true color vanished in the dim hall light. I searched high and low in the house, but she wasn't there, so I burst through the back door of the house to check the stable.

We hadn't gotten more than six inches of new snow the night before, so I more or less ran to the stable. White Horse was gone. Haunted, I walked to where he had lain. There was no blood on the ground, for his wounds had healed before he died to his dream of sweet alfalfa hay. So I didn't expect to find solid proof of his having been there. On the other hand, I was there. I was there. The hay was half eaten. There were tracks in the snow.

I followed the tracks to the front door of the whorehouse. The massive door was open. I heard music mixed with women's laughter, a thousand instruments strung on a thousand women, backed by a tinkling hum. Smelling the sour roses of the night before, thirsty for water, I walked over the porch, through the cavernous door, into The Beautiful Woman Without Mercy again.

There, plain as daylight on the flesh and bones of real people sat a hundred rovers against the walls of the parlor, and in their midst, Amy Survivor in the dead pilgrim wife's homespun calico dress, on the back of the pilgrims' White Horse. All the music stopped as her mouth smiled open and she spoke in a voice warm as tears, "Come over, Red Rover!"

I stepped toward her through a world of dead music and the dead eyes of rovers, helpless as a doll drawn by the thread of its unraveling, when a wan rover grabbed my foot with a grip as fierce as the Reaper's. I looked down at the face of a dead troubadour, a type I'd seen occasionally on the trail, perhaps No Future's face, but without a hat.

I kicked loose, pulled by the maiden, as on the back of the horse she rode out the cavernous doorway to the snow falling in flakes fat as hats onto the bare heads of the rovers who pursued her past death into the only street of The Town With No Name now buried under night falling in the form of darkness, no moon, no stars, and virgin snowflakes fat as drifting indigo straw hats falling through frozen time without a breath of air.

44

I woke up in the back of a buckboard bouncing along the old hard road that I knew from memory in the soles of my moccasins was the ancient grass-covered highway leading to Fate. Long before I'd met Jesus Green I'd walked many a mile there. The first thing I saw was crystal-blue sky, and the first thing I felt was sunshine on my face. Wrapped up tight in my sleeping style, sometimes called the swaddle fold, and my lips scum-shut underneath my snot-matted moustache and beard, I could neither move nor talk for the time being. So I just lay there and enjoyed being awake with no dream remembered.

I could tell my long winter's nap was over, for the air in my nostrils smelled of mud without the sting of snow; also, a robin sang its rare song from a tree off the road that I couldn't see for the sides of the buckboard, but knew was there by the song of the bird. A tear fell from my eye in the joy of life. From a time that may never have been I recalled a toddler lying in a real bed with blankets his own, peeking slowly out of them, through glass window panes, at the same blue sky. I cried harder, tears swelling both my eyes that burst in a torrent like clouds; and like the clouds, I don't know where in heaven the tears came from.

Then, unlike the clouds which seem in love with heaven, sometimes sinking close to earth in mountaintops and vales, but always returning to heaven, my tears might have spumed hot from the heart of hell, for as I blinked to clear them a distinct memory of Amy Survivor arose in the flow. I began to shiver in my swaddling clothes, and the matting over my mouth blew apart, as I pled with forgotten language to be unwrapped. Getting no response, I rolled in the wagon, like a caterpillar trying to shed its skin; but my wrap was too good. I couldn't shake free. I screamed, "Jesus!," a wagoneer's name. Finally I rolled onto my face and that's when I discovered the buckboard's real cargo: horse manure.

Believe it or not, I laughed. I laughed a long time, but the driver never turned around. Finally, I flipped back onto my back and just settled into the ride . . .

Along about dusk we rolled into Fate. I knew where we were since familiar buildings passed before my eyes as I peered up out of the horse manure. Also, a kid or two jumped aboard and peered down at my bone-thin face buried under the matted beard. As I smiled at them, they stared awestruck with amazement of the most genuine sort.

"I wish you were mine," I spoke weirdly, having been asleep so long, and they jumped off the wagon. I guess changes take place in a man while he sleeps, things no amount of dreaming can explain.

We pulled up to the sidewalk in front of a familiar roof, the

Nut House roof, but the name had been changed, according to the new sign burnt into oak that said, "Cornucopia," which I found out later means horn of plenty. I need not comment on that. But I will remark on how odd things fit back into place. I figure it may be due to the fact I'm one rover and trail's one trail. But that really explains very little and maybe nothing . . .

The driver was a short man, but not a midget, who had to reach up to unlatch the tailgate of the buckboard. At first I thought his fingers were those of a child reaching over the gate. (My head, having flipped over, was toward the tail-gate.)

He climbed up with a grunt onto the side of the wagon, and peered down familiarly into both my eyes, reeking of wal-nuts.

"You gonna unwrap me?" I asked with a surprising impa-tience and confidence a caterpillar has no reason to possess, but may.

Though he looked familiar, a jolly face nesting in an ancient beard topped by a sock hat, I was certain that we had never met. He smiled down at me and started signing language with his hands, making great gestures with his mouth and eyes, too. He pointed at his ears and crossed his fists, then he pointed at his throat and crossed his fists again. I knew he was speechless and couldn't hear, and I nodded as best I could, to let him know I understood. But he kept talking in his way, and I became increasingly impatient to get out of my wrap.

Then, as if to show me the worrisome fool I was, he pulled up his very long beard and pointed profoundly at a dogbite scar as long as a jackknife blade on his throat. It had healed without doctoring by any skilled hand. I could see that. It looked like a furrow slashed in mud and hardened. Then he pointed at my dead eye with his other hand, so that a living chain of flesh and bone was linking us, my dead eye to his dead throat, through his body. I wondered in dim horror if I might still be asleep, but dreaming.

Then he spryly and happily unwrapped me as if he'd understood my folding style since before it was invented by me, and as I lay there in my blankets over the fairly warm manure beginning to steam somewhat in the first of night, the two kids who'd jumped on the passing wagon earlier jumped up on the parked wagon. They looked at me unwrapped and rickety as I gradually sat up, first on my elbows, then on my seat, then pulled my knees up to my chest, folded my trembling arms around them, and sat there in the buckboard, looking around town to see what I could see from there.

It was the same old Fate. Nothing had changed but the season. But the kids weren't afraid to look at both my eyes.

Epilogue

I never saw my old pack or the personal items within it again. I forgave the person who stole it, figuring I had done just the same a thousand times, living off the fat of the land. I figured I shed that pack same as an oak sheds an acorn. Even if all that was not true, still I felt better thinking about it than I had when fantasizing ways to punish the thieving bastard if I ever found him. Also, I felt sure the pilgrim family in heaven would not find fault in my stealing their things; on the contrary, they probably didn't care . . .

I took a job spreading horse manure in Fate's municipal orchard. Fittingly, it was the same load of fertilizer that Jolly Wagoneer had hauled into town with yours truly in the pile. Through a series of rough drawings burned in the tea-fire of our encampment, admirable efforts to communicate, accompanied by his sincerest gestures in fingertalk I never understood, he finally made it clear to me that he had found me buried in an ancient steel buggy full of the very manure that he was paying me a twenty-pecan note to spread. That made sense, being as the manure was warm and it took a while to get the smell out of my blankets.

In turn, I drew pictures of the lazarus mouse, trying to tell him that story, since I was sure he was a man who could appreciate it. I also drew pictures by the tea-fire of life on the trail that I'd experienced, including a picture of Jesus Green, by which time we were communicating well, very few gestures involved.

Ultimately, over the last pot of tea we shared together before my savior moved on, I drew him a picture, the best of the bunch, of Amy Survivor on the back of her stallion, but Jolly Wagoneer could take no more. I guess there was too much meaning involved, or he just got fed up, because as soon as I drew in her squirrel eyes (they weren't even finished) he threw up his hands and retired to his bedroll under the buckboard.

I chose to sleep under the stars, shook the pine needles off my blankets, and spread out in the orchard. Sleep was sweet. I just melted with the manure into the roots of the apple trees. I never dreamed come morning the wagoneer would be gone, having left my twenty-pecan note in his poor scrip tucked in my coat pocket. I hoped it was cashable, since I'd lost my other.

The King of Scarecrows

Like a scarecrow in a cucumber field are they,
And they cannot speak;
They must be carried,
Because they cannot walk!
Do not fear them,
For they can do no harm,
Nor can they do any good.

— Jeremiah

1

We lived an inch from wild in those days. Me and Bobby and Dessa. With criminal backgrounds of little consequence, we worked the more austere, remote corners of the country.

As a threesome, we first came together in Blueknife, South Dakota, when I was thirty-one. Bobby went by the name "The Nobleman," a tattoo act. Dessa told fortunes, and I was The Human Scarecrow. In those days, freak shows traveled the face of the earth, but because of their ugliness were banned.

We met in Shorty Longhorn's trailer that fateful April night in Blueknife, S.D., each in search of a companion. At odd hours we had separately seen an advertisement tacked to the door of the Blueknife market; seeking an owner for a homeless dog, the author had snatched our eyes from roving over shelves of nourishment packed under beautiful lights, with words of glue and glitter. He had written: "PUPPY NEEDS HOME, ODD ROMANTIC ORIGIN, RED-LIGHT TRAILER, BLUEKNIFE TILL SUNDAY."

2

In those days, we moved on Sunday, when customers were in church or asleep . . . Sometimes by a river, like at a public park or under a tree, we'd pull off and worship together, either silently or reading out of the Bible.

Because Bobby could not read, not even the wise tattoos on his arms, and Dessa spent so much time in states of holy dread in the tent, readings often fell to me, and, sitting on a picnic table or fallen tree, I found the Family Bible in my hands. It had come to Dessa as payment from a farmer in Switching, Montana. It was white and floppy, and the gold was rubbed off the pages.

Once, as I read the Sermon on the Mount, whose meanings ring so clear I could lift my eyes off the page and still be reading, I glanced up at Bobby bare-armed in his overalls, standing on a fallen beech tree, with the jewel-blue Montana sky as a pillow-frame around him. My mouth and lungs kept reading, and Dessa reached over and held my hand. This left one hand for the Book.

3

Before continuing, I want it to be known that this is not a book. It is a man divided into chapters. The chapters arise out of ignorance, for lack of a better word, as have most of the movements of my life. However, faith is the road under my wheels at every turning, lit by a tendency to go too far.

4

Shorty's trailer was parked by a river that flowed through Blueknife, and, I suppose, still does. I know that it was not the Big Missouri, the longest river in America, but what it was called I fail to conjure back into memory.

The trailer was easy to find, since it was covered with strands of red carnival lights like you see on rides at night, all except the tractor to which the trailer was attached for immediate hauling at the drop of a hat.

I came upon the marvel at dusk on a Saturday night, knowing he was due to pull out the next day. The big tractor engine was running smooth as silk, like an expert clock running into eternity, and it got louder and louder as I approached. Ultimately, when I felt the wonderful heat of the engine, I stopped in the dirt and read the black and gold wording on the side of the trailer (the whole rig was red): "Shorty Longhorn's Traveling Curiosities . . . The Weirdest World on Wheels." It gave me a glow like a person remembering home. I walked around the rig, looking under it and all around.

Night had fallen on the river, whose sound the engine drowned.

After rapping on the rear door of the trailer and getting no answer, I stepped up onto the running board of the vibrating tractor and peered inside through the open shotgun window. I saw this odd-appearing gentleman asleep on the seat, lighted by the dashboard lights augmented by a certain amount of red light toning in through the windows. I say he was odd-appearing because he had the features of a dwarf but was big. Curled up there, he looked like a huge infant suffering through a dream. He had fallen asleep with a stovepipe hat on his head, into which a great thick flow of cotton-fine blond hair had been stuffed; the hat had tumbled off the seat onto the floor with a bunch of hair still in it.

I sort of feared waking him, as I fear waking anyone, but especially a stranger, so I very gently stepped down from the truck and walked away.

Up on the road I had seen a path cutting through trees down to the river, and I took that path, hoping that in time he would wake up. Walking alongside the river and occasion- ally glancing back to find the red lights shining through the trees, I began to worry that everything was now spoiled, that my path in life was de-charmed, since I had failed to awaken him.

Feeling chilled by a blanket of air that slipped off the river and covered me, I spun away to shake it off, and hurried back to where the path met the road, just as a woman passed in a long shawl and jangling bracelets. Some straw fell from me in the wind she made.

5

The musky wind behind her smelled something like licorice and roses. Her gait was tall and graceful. She walked how people walk in dreams . . .

I followed a distance behind her to Shorty's trailer, and saw Shorty climb down from the cab to greet her. He looked pretty glad though she towered above him. She stood very erect with her arms crossed under the shawl. Due to the drone of the engine they had not heard my footsteps in the otherwise silent evening, and I paused, hanging back in the darkness, to watch and see if they made a deal. That being the case, I wouldn't have to suffer through an introduction; I could go my separate way . . .

But, no, quite soon he fetched a lantern from the truck and hung it from a tripod under a leafless tree. He brought out two folding chairs, and he and the woman sat down. Because of the red lights I knew that this was the trailer with the dog, but I wanted to go away. Around them sitting by the lantern, I felt the magnetic threat, or terror, of knowing other folks . . .

Pretty soon, another person passed me like I wasn't even there. I had taken the position of a shadow, and felt good about it, when the man wearing elegant evening clothes rushed by. I checked for his odor, but he had none. As he greeted the regal woman seated like a gypsy queen, the big dwarf ran to the trailer for another chair.

6

Some wind blew up, but as my coat was packed with straw I didn't feel it. I also had straw in the pockets of my pants. I had learned through experience how to stuff my clothing in such a way as to minimize losses, though everywhere I went I left pieces of my costume like a trail . . .

The wind came up, but I didn't much feel it. Magnificently, I felt increasingly a shadow of the tree beneath which I stood captive of the sight of the two men and woman seated by the lantern. I keep thinking it was a pine . . .

Like the wind which dies down and blows up, in turns and always, the terror I felt at possibly meeting these people suddenly evaporated into a lesser, quite comfortable feeling of safety. I think I shut my eyes and napped for a while, when, awakened by whining and two kinds of laughter, I saw the dwarf standing under the lantern that swung in the wind, and the tall man and woman gaily petting the animal the dwarf held in his arms.

Drawn towards the new quartet like a handful of straw in the wind, I withdrew from the safety of the pine and advanced very slowly. I guess I would've looked like an animated dead man, a stick dude in preacher's frock, a scarecrow to the queen as she, with her white hand on the animal, looked up smiling from the hood of her shawl.

7

As the wind died down I heard hiding in the waves of engine noise the wailings of a mongrel preacher. On Saturday night in Blueknife, somebody was screaming the Gospel.

It brought back a flood of memories from youth when Dad, a salesman of magic lubricants, Bibles, and insurance, dragged our family from community to community looking for that pot of gold. Everywhere we'd go, we'd join a different church. It wasn't planned. Dad found a preacher he liked and if they let him and Mom smoke on the lawn before church, we went there.

You don't forget that beautiful look of a man in a blue suit smoking alongside other parishioners, or with his wife, or by himself, in the clear sunlight of Sunday, while inside the music's blowing up and the organist makes perfect mistakes . . .

I had spoken something forgettable and some straw had fallen from my sleeve when my mind drifted back to the moment and I said, "Nice to meet you" to the elegant, mustachioed gentleman shaking my hand.

"I hate the name 'Bob,'" he said. "Everybody has it."

"Ah! An honest nobleman!" the dwarf announced, and passed me a bottle of whiskey. "And you, my friend," he said. "You must be — the Scarecrow Preacher!"

Wishing to keep my identity a secret, I said nothing exactly and took a deep drag off the bottle. The whiskey burned in my hollow chest like the hay in my vest was on fire.

8

I don't like it when things get too personal. Who you are and where you come from is nobody's business. I felt identically, then, too.

9

Except for some extreme differences in appearance, i.e., size and shape of limbs, digits, and face, the big dwarf and the Nobleman could've been relations. In the lantern glow their fine blonde hair was the same color.

Best way to put it is that the dwarf's fine blonde hair looked like a very rich cottonball stuffed expertly into his stovepipe hat.

The tall Nobleman's mane was very fine, baby-fine, and thin, and hung down to his chin from where it had fallen off his ears like a rhyme to his long mustache. A very articulate, gleeful fellow, he appeared. His warm handshake was richly informed with experience. He had no tattoos below the cuffs or above the collars. Of course, at that introductory moment I didn't know he was a tattoo act. He looked more like a wandering thespian.

As for the weird madonna to my right with her hand on the dog of odd romantic origin, she looked like a gypsy queen from a blackened clan, more Celt than Romany, tall and stern as a white tree wrapped in black cloth. When I passed her the bottle, she didn't touch my hand, and I was glad. Her bangles jangled tune-like, all silver high up her white-sapling arm.

As the ignorant dwarf did not bring a cup from his truck for her, the Nobleman offered a collapsible cup from his coat pocket, which she took and held while he poured the whiskey into it for her to drink. I admired his grace, but secretly wished she had placed her dark lips upon the bottle where I had.

10

The reason we had come together was the dog, but I have decided not to describe it. Leave it said, it was the ugliest creature God ever let pass between the portals of a womb. It drew instant pity, even from a straw man. However, its lack of beauty prevented it from being picked from a litter or, in worst case scenario, from a cardboard box by any man with eyes. It was so ugly even a blind man would have winced upon feeling of it for a picture. I reached across the darkness of our bodies, though, and rubbed its mane. It snort-whimpered, and hare-lipped me.

I had petted a child's cat earlier at dinner in town. The dog was sure as hell of milk, and I'd say nine months old, as its orange tongue damn near wrapped around my wrist, though a fairly narrow gauge, as it tried to lick off the cat smell.

"A puppy, eh?" the Nobleman said. He was not being cruel, for if the big dwarf loved the monster, why was he giving it up?

In answering the Nobleman, the man just laughed.

We sat in four camp chairs, looking at the dog for awhile. Its eyes of marbled satin caught some light. I listened for the Preacher's voice in the idling of the truck but could not hear it. Some little tidbits passed among us I can't remember.

There was a smidgen of liquor left in the bottle, and the dwarf let the puppy lick it out. It snorted with glee, its lightning tongue long to the bottom.

I sat back straight in my chair, but the veiled woman reached in horror for the babe wiggling in the big dwarf's arms.

11

It was called the Sawgut. The river that cut through
Blueknife. It just dawned on me.

12

We split up and went our separate ways. Well into the night, as it grew chill, and after all the tales were told, there fell a sharp stillness over the red encampment. I felt them look at me, and I stood up and left. It was not that they were not cordial. They were. It was just that when the wind went to sleep the dwarf's magnificent rig was also silent. It had run out of gas. The picture in my mind of those carnival lights growing dim drew blood from my eyes, and I saw spots. "My cue to go," I said, and they said a few pleasant things.

13

In my tent that night I dreamed I stood on the ground by a low-roofed sod farmhouse and watched six children play some sort of tag on the roof. The roof was thatched. The rows of thatch looked like a thousand broom-heads God had woven.

Three of the children were "undecided"; they walked onto the left side of the roof. The other three, all girls, danced gaily to the right. One of the gay ones had white-blonde hair in long pigtails. The sky around her and the rest was prairie blue and felt like a melting star in love with this earth.

I had never seen her before, and I was not asleep, when someone called my name. As I was empty, I had just lain down in my straw-packed clothes and gone to sleep, awaking only to dream, when my name was called at the door of the tent and I got up to see who was there.

It was the gypsy woman. I unzipped the fly and invited her in. Refusing politely, she said that she was sorry to disrupt my sleep but there was no other way to catch me before daylight and we all hit the road.

My mouth was dusty, my throat full of hay. I was drunk but still had my boots on. I wondered why she was there.

"I hope it's alright," she said, and opened her great shawl to show me the basket of straw she had there. The dog must've been buried in there.

"Sure," I said. And she went away . . .

When I lay back down, the children were gone from the roof. My naked feet sunk in the mossy-cold earth to my an-kles.

14

I would like to describe for you the feeling of getting up at dawn on Sunday in April, and you're in your own tent, wearing your own clothes, and when you step outside to stretch and see your old junky truck with its doghouse-type shelter built on the back with wood and nails and shingles, you feel the chill of all the promises living makes, you suck it in, it feels good all the way down to your empty stomach, like a river of ice water percolating in your lungs, and you look at the pine tree beneath which millions of scarecrows have camped, and up the green ribbon of river that takes everything and gives it back, then turn barefoot in the cold dust and watch it flow sadly away, and say its name, "Sawgut," because it's here and you are standing in South Dakota, you've driven ten steel stakes into South Dakota, made holes that time, dirt, and the river will heal, but I can't do so satisfactorily.

It is better just to say I got up at dawn and tore down camp, put it in the truck, and took off looking for a cafe for breakfast, the bare sticks of Sunday like a sleeping sycamore.

The hardwoods had not yet leafed out, though the conifers were green.

I looked at my feet in the dust, and wondered who'd taken my boots off.

15

I drove barefoot in my truck a few miles upriver to the town of Frisco, where I found the Frisco House B & B. I thought a B & B was a kind of drink, but the kind woman who let me come in barefoot said it meant Bed and Breakfast.

At that time in this country, the bed and breakfast was a brand new phenomenon. At one time, they were just nice houses where old maids and widows lived, a sort of special category without a title . . .

They had a heraldic crest built into the backs of the chairs in the dining room, and over the fireplace they'd mounted the full-size heraldic shield with three Latin words on it painted gold. Though I had gone to school various places and times, and had read some books on my own, my Latin was dust and I couldn't resurrect it, so as I stared through breakfast time at the full-size crest up on the fireplace the kind woman who had welcomed me as a preacher without shoes told me she had bought the chairs and the full-size crest "back East, in Pawtucketville," a phrase I have carried with me like a postcard ever since. I don't know why. Some things just stick in your mind like a fleck of broomstraw driven through a telephone pole by a tornado.

"They were first owned by the Herlihee family of Massachusetts," she said. "Work . . . Suffer . . . Love," she said, and poured me more tea water into a pot modelled after a cat.

I had had my choice of teas from a basket hidden under daffodils on the table where she seated me, and I'd picked the Gunpowder. It tasted like peas and piss boiled together.

She seemed happy with my choice, and tucked a ribbon-tied package of Gunpowder tea into the pocket of my coat.

16

It was one of those Sundays when suddenly you realize it's Easter.

Nobody else came for breakfast but me, and the kind lady vanished into the kitchen.

I turned in my chair to face the street where my truck was parked. I saw it through a window.

The night past, the gypsy queen had left the doghouse door open when she had come to get straw for her dog, for now the door was ajar and sunlight shone on the hay.

All my sweet clover hay I cherished from year to year was in there. What I saw now was the last cutting from spring a year before, hand-harvested with a sickle in Hay, Texas, the best hay country in the world. I am not a man to cry, but it was a religious experience, as some of the hay was till green.

"You should have seen the boy who picked it," I said, as if to my companion.

That's when a family of people walked by on their way to church. The girl and mother both wore pink, the boy and his father blue. In their bonnets they had woven wild lilies, and the boys had bootineers. The man and boy held hands as they walked, and so did the mother and girl. The boy turned his head to look at my truck, but the man's attention never veered off the path to church.

"Farmers," I said . . .

A few minutes later I got up to pay, but the woman wouldn't take my money. "It's Easter," she said, like it was Christmas.

I went out to my house and shut the back door securely; I thought of my house as having three doors. That's when the kind old woman ran outside after me with a sackful of shoes in her hands. They had belonged to her husband, and she was giving them to me.

17

I followed the Sawgut River west and set up camp before dusk. It was a grove of pines off the road, with water and restrooms. The State of South Dakota is good about its transient population . . .

I remember wishing I had a Bible to look at or hold in my hands by the firehole where a thousand other men in hand-me-downs had pondered the future and where to go next. "No," I spoke to the stars in the heavens hid above the pines. I had to hear my own voice because it proved I had a soul, an answer . . .

Lacking a Bible, I put the sack of widow's shoes on my lap, and held it. Above the sunken firehole I could see my truck-house at rest; breathing long, deep, and slowly, I smelled the clover hay above the smell of pine.

I swear that if I had not needed the sweet hay for my work, I would have eaten it all like a horse. But with sweet clover you don't have to bathe or wash your clothes so often, and your rolling home smells good. After you're grown, the closest thing to home is the smell of it . . .

I fell asleep by the fire, which for a scarecrow is dangerous. But the good thing is you never dream, so you never move, and when you wake up you're always where you were the night before. The same holds true for a nap, anywhere. But the best thing is, when you wake up it's Monday, or not Sunday, you hope.

18

I should say a scarecrow dreams, but never asleep. Holding the sack of shoes by the fire that first night out of Frisco, I woke by opening my eyes to the crackle, and saw the six children feeding the hole with fresh pine. The boughs sent up impermanent stars and the children stayed speechless. The girls were on one side (to the right), the boys to the other. I watched them for a moment, then went back to sleep.

19

In the morning the fire was dead. I pulled a wing-tip shoe from the sack and poked the fire corpse to see if I could stir up some hot life, but the one-time warm and whispering companion was gone.

"He's gone," I said.

Determined to make something happen, I drew a line in the dirt like Jim Bowie, and wrote the four letters for the four directions around the points of the cross where you always see them. Then I stopped to think. Then I drew a straight line intersecting my main (first) line at the far-western end, forming half a box. I felt something happening. I wrote the word *Nebraska* west of the second line. Tears flooded my eyes and dripped onto the dirt, forming the source of the Sawgut River on the Black Hills toe of the widow's wing-tip shoe which had been her husband's.

"It's mine," I thought. "The plan, the shoe, everything."

I heard something rumbling far off, then closer, and afraid I was being found out, I put the shoe in the sack and scratched out the map. The feeling was the one you get when the most precious things in the world are dragged away.

The rumble burst into a drumming concussion. It became suddenly impossible not to know. I smelled the blood of the grass and the other delicate perfumes cut by the farts of the monster.

Tucking my guts into my vest, I stood with my green pine stick and saw the State of South Dakota tractor cut the virgin grass along the road west of Frisco. I could've reached from my truck and touched the mower's arm where it hung so relaxed.

20

Driving barefoot is dangerous, especially if the rubber's worn off your clutch.

As the mist burnt off the river, I washed my feet and found a mossy place to dump the widow's shoes: six pair, including the black wing-tips. These were farmer's footwear worn over a period of decades. It made me thirsty just to look at them.

I took the Nobleman's collapsible cup, which I had accidentally stolen, and scooped up some of the Sawgut and sipped it.

"Better than that gunpowder shit," I stated, feeling the wealth well up in my bones like rainwater in sticks. It was the wealth of rivers and leather every scarecrow knows.

21

The wing-tips fit perfectly, and they went with my suit. If the mower had seen me before I put them on (which he had not), he would have thought me an insane preacher put out with a sackful of food. Just putting on the widow's shoes made me out to be more human, wholer . . .

About this time, I wished I had a watch or calendar, for outside proof it was indeed Monday. On the other hand, I was out of pocket money, so I packed up camp (I had pitched a tent but not slept in it) and pulled out, following my river.

There wasn't a car on the highway. I could go as slow as I wanted, and stop on bridges to look at the sundancing waters. The river would disappear into trees, then reoccur a mile down the road.

As I drove, I dreamed of the girl with the white-blonde hair, laughing on the farmhouse roof. The green boughs with which she fed and beat the fire rhymed with the trees that rimmed the river like a loose green ribbon through her hair. I think she saw me, too.

I'll never know how much time passed before the next sun-down hit me like a widow's glove at the border of Wyoming, the Equal Rights State, but I felt it with the windows down. It was a cold kid glove, a farmer's gauntlet.

"I wish I had that ugly-ass dog with me," I said, rolling up the window and closing the vents.

22

In the dark, surrounded by young fields that would need scarecrows, even with the windows up I could smell the range of mountains way away. The names Medicine Bow and Bighorn come back like two big crows on my shoulders . . .

I flashed my brights at the black road and swerved left and right in an effort to see the ghosts of soldiers, Indians, and pioneers inhabiting the flattened places. Anything for company . . . You'd think they needed it, considering the sparse population . . .

Bill, Dogie, and Dull Center, the towns through which I passed that night, had a combined population of 50. I wrote their numbers on the sole of a deerskin shoe.

As I searched for work that pitch-dark Wyoming Monday night, through three dark towns, I kept the shoe next to me, against my leg, and sang of Natty Bumppo. Next to human company and human things, animal company and animal things, human and animal angels and their songs make good company.

Ghosts, already lonely and lacking confidence, irritate and fail to console . . . But a ghost, you will find, is better than nothing.

23

Somewhere west of Bill that night I nodded off. Usually when that happens I don't wreck for some reason, and this was no exception. It always happens that I get so tired of dreaming, I have to sleep. Also, fear and worry seem to run through the grain of my framework, and they make me fall asleep. "The black aspirin," my father called it.

Somewhere west of Bill I fell asleep with the windows down in my truck. Fortunately, it was at the moment I ran out of gas, since the three gas stations in Dull Center, Dogie, and Bill had closed by the times I got there, and I just glided off the road into some grass on a flattened place. Sometimes I marvel to think of all the lives the glaciers saved . . .

Sometime in the night I stirred to the strains of a gypsy violin drifting and dancing through the black margin, and I got out to piss on the rocks. I found the hill of rocks there when I stepped out. Evidently, my truck had rolled up to that hill and gently stopped. I climbed the hill and peed on top under an arbor of stars big as roses.

The violin music might have spontaneously exploded from the hay-manure for brains a scarecrow has, but when I opened my black-button eyes atop that hill I saw at first like a fiery rose at my feet, then as what it was: the boys and girls dancing round a fire down in the canyon. These were the six children.

Though I tried to see the one from the other, and the white-blonde girl among the rest, I failed.

Refusing to risk a complete loss of margin, and needing my sleep, I clambered back down to my truck.

24

Back in the truck I could not go back all the way to sleep. Drifting over the hill like milk over a breast, the gypsy violin fed my dream of the girl I never met nor knew before the six-children-dancing farmhouse dream back yonder.

"A new life . . . a new creature," I mentioned aloud to Wyoming.

25

Back in those days, anything was possible. You felt like, eventually, everything would happen.

About dawn I was awakened completely into Tuesday by a wandering, doddering old minstrel toting a sack of wild onions which brushed my shoulder as he jogged past the truck and spooked a strange little deer on the hill.

After the old tunester was gone over the hill, the little deer tip-toed back with dew on its nose and hay in its mouth, and sniffed the hood of my truck.

As for the old minstrel, he has nothing to do with anything. Anybody, a deer, a woman, a child, a stray horse, could have run by with those onions.

26

Well, it was Tuesday and I had no job. My truck was out of gas about ten miles west of Bill.

The deer kept sniffing around for hay, and because I sat so still behind the wheel of the truck the brazen animal actually felt obliged or welcome to nibble the stuffing from my sleeve. This produced in me the dream of being completely consumed by grazing animals, deer, antelope, buffalo and mice nuzzling, rooting, whipping, digging and crawling through my clothes till there was nothing left to hang on a stick; my clothes lay strewn across a hilly pasture under the great Montana sky.

"Why not Wyoming?" I spoke in the dream, or from it, and the little deer sniffed up my arm to my neck, nibbled a long hay-stem there, pulled it out (golden Johnsongrass), shook it in the stillness of morning, and backed away from the door.

I looked at him. He stepped forward and sniffed the buttons of my eyes.

189

28

Sometimes you get the feeling things are coming to an end, like a river flowing towards a waterfall, but you're wrong. It's just the rumble of existence echoing up the canyon housing a turn.

I had that feeling about sundown as I approached within reading distance a little green sign on a white post by the road: Tin Cup, no population. I stopped a few feet away, and read it closely.

I looked around at the fields and buttes and some mountain range far away, all wild, without fences. There had been fences, but they were trampled down. I could see for miles in every direction. No house nor shed nor building, even in ruins, stood anywhere.

"This can't be," I thought silently, since Tin Cup was where I was born.

29

But I didn't have time to feel sorry for myself, which I really enjoy, because I was starving to death, out of work, and in desperate need of companionship. If I didn't watch it, I'd fall asleep and never wake up again.

"Dream on," I heard someone say. I looked all around at the glaciated, rock-rutted graveyard of Tin Cup around me, a town that used to be, and deduced it had to be me.

Tuesday, I guessed, was only a shadow of Monday, and Monday of Sunday . . . I was losing my mind, as they say, "going haywire". . . when I heard wings beating, as if drumming out a soldier of the corps, the soft drumming of a goatskin of air by the hands of an angel . . . and, throwing my head back to the heavens, I saw a great black crow's feet folded on its belly, and the black beak and hat-pin eyes, as its soft, ribbed wings beat my face — like a woman's or kind father's blessed soft hands cupping fleetingly the child's face — and I fell back to earth, like a fainting woman or a man without muscle, fast asleep . . .

I awoke to gray light and complete stillness. It was a joyous weakness. I wallowed in it without moving. Then, I had to move because something was wiggling under my knee.

I laughed, and rolled, and when I rolled onto my side three crows hopped off me and beat their wings like black gulls hovering.

"They think I'm dead," I thought, so I sat up straight in the road to prove I wasn't. They flew away.

My head filled with blood as the sun rose above a hill and I heard it crackling. This happened however fast the sun moves to hold the earth and the earth rolls toward it.

Since the birds were gone, I lay back down on the road and heard a humming rumble. Whatever it was, it had to stop or kill me. I lay stock still to wait for haven.

"Woo," I whispered.

With my eyes shut in a dream I remembered my father standing on some bricks with his violin. "The homeplace," I said, and heard the tune in part, as the rumble blew into a roar and I reached for the fiddle.

30

The next thing I saw was the word *Fragile* on a cardboard box, one of many lining the inside of a shed. Beautiful daylight surrounded the door of the shed. It was dead silent for a moment, then I heard flute music and the feet of a woman approaching. She and the music were detached . . .

The door opened violently with a sucking rush, but didn't slam, and the Queen of Gypsies entered on the smell of licorice and roses burning in the sun. She rushed up to me so that our noses almost touched, so that those invisible feelers on our noses touched, and looked very boldly and wild into my button-black eyes. Then she looked at my torn mouth, licked her own lips, licked mine, shut her eyes, and kissed me . . .

"Only the beginning," she said, with her eyes shut, and I believed her, but as she pricked a piece of hay from her cheek her eyes flew away like birds or fish with wings in her head, and I wondered what she meant.

All I could do was hang there. I hadn't even held her. She backed away and opened her shawl and showed me a thousand bills. Money.

"One night!" she whispered. "One night!" I thought that I grinned but her face got wilder. "You're too believable, incredibly believable," she said.

31

Antwerp, Chantilly, Flox, Steubenville, Hector, Tom, Lust, Glorious Divide, Carson City, Zone, Figure Eight, Robber's Rest, Ventricular, Integrity, Honorville, Waupekong, Minominee, Zero Interest, Comfort, Nemo, Parsons, Cherry Lake, Flathead, Indianapolis, Gorgeous, Tuffs Corner, Heroic, Six Points, Three Rivers, Regular, Fix, Why Not, Rounder, Horse, Ap, Liggon, Russet, Sweetpea, Hartack, French, Susanville, Susie, Rigorous, Bait, Big Spruce, Lodgepole, Hunger, Mary's Mesa, Pseudo Gap, Blockhead, Harness, Holy Hell, Heaven, Heaven-I-Think, Heaven Again, (two Heavens), Flirty, Red Saddle, Whyso, Dao, Linda, Nancy, Ding, Ferocious, One Paw, Fletcher, Zinc, Bartholomew, Happy Tit, Uncertain, Worsen, Pit, Fit, Video, Play's-the-Thing, Ranger, Saxxy, Pyrite, Dairy Center, Dillville, Hope, Maybe, Shoulda, Sixgun, Colt, Navy, Bullet, Weir, Old Tom, Hank, TV, Morose, Morocco, Dry Wash, Marisco, Artist, Swig, Petunia, Uno, Fartston, Bleery, Megalode, Copper, Simple, Keisternoggen, Wonderlust, Pancho, Pampa Puree, Cranfills Gap, Rough Nugget, Hall, Ruby, Rude Kitty, Doc, Furious, New Kokomo, Paul's Valley, Plummet, Marble Steep, Crustaisha, Hot Creek, Cottonwood, Parlayview, Minnie's Camp, Wish-I-May, Harterville, Such, Reality (Mont.), No Shit, Fog,

Francios, Second Streak, Indian Luck, Crazy Dog, Lost, No
Buddhist, Question Mark, Tangible, One Ireland (Id.),
Hatred, Prospect, Bonanza, Hoss, Little Joe, Hop Sing
(Tex.), My Linda, Forget-me-not, Blackeye, Higgs, Funny
Lady, Missus, Where (N.M.), Manitoba, Twice, Sanger,
Nightly, Confucious, Was, Rio-no-rio, Watch it, Smoky,
Refugio, Back-to-Back, La Honda, Blackjack, Truchas,
Signet City, Wolf City, two Nevadas, Fiasco, Fleugerville,
Pleased, Davenport, Swisher, Humidor, Clubhouse, Velvet,
Center, Russian Lock, Tweezer, Happy Family, Lignite,
Mix, Jennifer's Landing, Trailhead, Engelmann, Iota, Dot,
New Dot, Jilson, Sacia's Orchard, Fux, Poor Grendel,
Depression, Manic, Jungston, Freud (Ark.), Unity Church
(Cal.), Papalote, Mangus, Rerun, Bleechville, Sardonic,
Search, Chillout, Coldspot, Bomber, Jester Beach, LaHood,
Badger, More, Meunster, Corpus Christi (Cal.), Lucky
Strike, Vigoroso, El, Zen-no-more, Just, Carp Creek, La
Orange, Hopeso, Pescadero, Miz Fontaine, Chocolate
Mountain, Olier, Arrivederci, El Salto, Laughter,
Pumpkinville, Deville, Castro, Olivet, Personality,
Marmalade, Plain Jane, Steve, Neophyte, Peterville,
Mainframe, Glyph, Shortness, Misty Land, Bagette,
Threesome, Baby's Head (Tex.), Meander-not, Monitor,
Mink, Sweet Water, Worst Case, Unbug, Buddyville,
Loudmouth, Forgiveness, Martha, Marfa, Moppola, Dry
River, Wall, Rag Doll Pass, Little Mo, Frandy, Fraley, Frick,
Duvall, Wick, Was It, Matilly, Chanteuse, Try Harder,
Beep, Hanjobber, Little Susie, Graphic Smile, Hardy's Boy,
For John (Calif.), Hardeehar (Ore.), Nonplussed, Fearsome
Corner, Badsay, Baggit, Burnt Case, Encyclopedic
Knowledge (Id.), Ten Homesteads, Ink, Deadpan, Freaks
Camp, Achia, Pokerface, Feelings, Granny Smith,
Grampa's Uke, plain Uke, Virginity, Harlot, Lake du loc,

Hell (a ghost town), Girly, Weemer, Sally, Hope-it's-a, Secrecy, Hiding Place, Fun, Campagna, Browner, Soliloquy, Kyd's Revenge, Spanish, plain Spain (Ok.), True Believer, Corn Center (where I escaped briefly), Oakford, Mulberry, Most, Mickey, Wore Out, Jimmy, Willyville, Zest.

32

None too sacred, these towns. For two days I've thought about their names. Where has it gotten me?

Dave, Medicine Hat, Thumbhorn, Vike . . . Whitehorse, Dawson, Prologue, Tok . . . Anitaville, Big Rita, Honduras (Alaska), Greyling, Esther . . . Zinc Spot, Gene, Abandonment, Fritz.

Oh, Lord, the smell of perfume on the streets of those places! It never belonged, so was blown up to the stars that lit our faces, tents, and plates when they were empty. Food is an agreement to go on, hay or hamburger, waiting to be taken up. And when I'd licked the tin plate clean, I'd taste the cold stars on it, and naturally remember home, some pie made of aspects, the roof, the dinner take, the sky.

"Tin pie," I said one night after closing a big weekend in Maidenville. It was way down the line. We'd been together as a troop for quite a while. I don't know. Years maybe. Certainly, years in the end.

O'Dessa, Robert, Shorty, the dog, and I had done our

Saturday night Bible reading after closing "the Hut" at Maidenville, Alberta, and we ate beans and wieners with seven-grain bread under a public shelter roof housing picnic tables from the sky. The sides were open.

Somebody said something funny, and everybody laughed. "You laughed, Scarecrow!" Dessa exclaimed. She sounded like a little girl who'd never known a man, nor yet been hurt by one.

"That's great!" the Nobleman refrained. His voice was pierced by real, unimaginary experiences of willful violence for money, such as when he burnt down the home for way-ward children in Meeganville, S.D., shortly before joining the show. There was no note of sorrow in his voice, and we all knew he had done other things.

Shorty was drunk.

The dog smiled. By then the mongrel was fat, still young but with a successful show. He was dubbed Lord Byron the Dog Prince of Newstead Abbey, due to his eyes, mainly. "Those eyes!" O'Dessa used to say, squeezing Byron's cheeks as he dozed on her lap; then, with a thrusting thrill and quake of her shoulders she'd lay a big kiss on his muz-zle. This prompted Robert to take off his clothes and flash his tattoos in the lamplight. It was an intricate act involving numerous contortions and "friezes" which he took from various traditions learned from pictures. These pictures he kept in his trunk stowed in Shorty's van. (We called the main part of the carnival truck "the Van.") . . .

Seeing O'Dessa kiss Lord Byron sickened Shorty to the ex-tent he closed his eyes and pushed away like a man sick of food, and he strolled away. The tongue business with the gypsy laughing fascinated Robert and he stood near them showing his penultimate tattoo: a tiny rose and a snake on its thorny stem, green and red and black on the end of his penis.

I turned up the lantern light to see it better, for this was a once-in-a-lifetime thing (though he showed this to those who could pay in every town I've named, plus others). Robert wasn't excited in the normal way. Because an artist at his trade, he just posed, and said calmly like Adonis or Michelangelo's David if the marble could talk, not even looking at us, his eyes like Christmas balls glimmering in Coleman lantern light: "Snake and Rose," the final segment of his act.

I looked at it closely. "Where'd you get it done?" I asked. Understand, I hadn't talked in years.

Dessa let up. "I did it," she said proudly. "Free," she added.

It had been finely wrought.

33

It was normal for us, and Shorty seemed good-hearted. On some nights he let youths in free to have their palm read and watch the Nobleman disrobe. Even free, these were not quickie acts . . .

Somehow, though, people always had money. Even in Spectreville, where the silver had run out twenty years before, a dozen or so citizens showed up with money.

The Nobleman's palms were tattooed, and he'd say to some awestruck shepherdess: "If you will place something in it, I will show you my hand." Money, he meant. She'd take a coin out of her jeans, and Bobby would open one hand to show a pink rose. The shepherdess would giggle, want to see the other hand and produce another coin. Slowly, as if engrossed in revelation, Bobby would open the other hand to show a coiled-up snake with a red tongue flickering.

Sometimes, as in Prudence, Montana, on a Friday night when the customers were gone, the same shepherdess would come back for Bobby's final act. It would be a private showing in the trees, followed by a swim in the river.

Sometimes O'Dessa did similar tricks. For instance, she told a lonely old shepherd from Particulate that if he, a generous man, wasn't careful, some foul fortune would suck him in; only the gypsy's kiss could change this fortune by removing all the shadows from his palm. He agreed, and the gypsy queen "kissed" his palm and the fingers attached. The old shepherd lost consciousness, and she sucked off all his shadows.

Sometimes the wails around camp were sweeter than owls' cries or birds' weeping. These services always seemed normal in those days. Now, as age advances and has advanced, they seem more supernatural . . .

Even I participated in charity shows. As I hung on my stick in a tent or a cellar, sometimes a shed or a barn, Shorty would let folks in free to interview me, gawk like giddy crows, and fondle my vestments to see if I'd move. For, ever since the day he hit me on the road at Tin Cup, I'd had trouble standing, talking, smiling, and moving. But it was the heart of my act, and brought in the bucks. Lord knows how many thousands of dollars have been tucked into the pockets of my vest!

34

All this money was turned over to Shorty and kept in "the hole" in his truck. I never saw this place. Most of the time, I dwelt in solitude like a doll cast aside.

It wasn't bad. O'Dessa would hold me and sing gypsy songs in a language I didn't understand. Even if I had understood it, I couldn't write it down, now, notes and all . . .

Still, my sense of smell remained keen. At night in the summer once in Pocket Mouse, Montana, after a big hay harvest, the smells of the farmgirls gussied up with shampoos and perfumes, powders and straw hats with flowers (a contest where the girls picked their own), combined with the odors of Robert's *eau de lilac* and hot O'Dessa's usual licorice rose, caused me to lose consciousness and fall utterly asleep on my rack.

Had some thugs from Missoula not stripped me of my clothing in search of blood money — the earnings of farmers searching for mystery — I might never have awoken. It was not their violent rifling that awoke me, however, but O'Dessa's fingers gently caressing the bone of my thigh, and weeping tears that fell off her black lips on it, and her singing one of those foreign-language melodies. It was so soft and romanesque that milk seeped eventually from my thigh.

Why, not even the wind or direct air had touched my legs (for they bathed me blindfolded) (they bathed me wrapped in a white sheet Shorty had from antiquity), and now here I hung with her breath on me.

35

One night a group of boys stole me and took me to an old man who fed me liquor. He said he wanted to mortify me.

The boys were not privy to his wish, and I knew not what to say. This may have been before I spoke the words "Tin pie" after the life-changing accident . . . It was . . .

Anyway, I sat with the old man all night, till morning when he took me back to camp in his cattle truck and pinned ten dollars to my hat and dropped me off. The boys had smuggled me out the back of the tent through an emergency exit, and that's where Old John left me . . .

Old John, that was his name. The poor drunk's name just drifted back to me on the smell of cowshit and hay baked on the floor of the truck.

36

You can dig up dirt on even the finest men, and Shorty was no different.

I know he took my earnings, but I never objected. Being considerably older, he called me "Son" and "Pal" and treated me pretty much like family. He somehow fed me with whatever it is the big dwarfs have — soul, maybe, that sweet fire, the basic note you smell on the breath of babies and old people sick or not — I'll call it the invisible bread of life, whose twin might be the grass that bleeds into the other bread. I don't know.

I don't know much other than shit and hay and rags and what they did for me, for the bread inhabited them . . .

But here's what happened to Shorty. We'd played Dreadnaught, British Columbia, six nights in a row; it was Saturday midnight sharp. I was down in the river, bathing in the sheet and net, with Bobby Topanga and O'Dessa Herlihee attending to see I did not float away, for this was the mighty Teslin.

It had been a dead night, as we had drained the population of loggers, trappers, nature guides, a holy man of the cloth and a couple of whores, and the usual collection of pioneers — eccentrics from elsewhere, tourists of normalcy, drifters, a history teacher from Seattle panning for gold — over the five days previous. In fact, all we'd fleeced that night was a band of Hoosier boys in a camper bound for Alaska, one of whom loved the Queen of Gypsies . . .

After bathing me, they dried me on a rock and left me to rest in the moonlight while they frolicked in the river, laughing and gasping. Then they climbed up the rocks (great white boulders like loaves of bread) and packed me back into my clothes and helped me back up the fir-studded, steep slope to the state site where the show was stationed under a big, open-sided rotunda, like an old band shelter.

When we got there, only the Hoosier boy who loved the Queen of Gypsies stood beneath the dome by Shorty Longhorn's lantern light. He had a big rag soaked in lineament wrapped around his neck, and a month's beard, and he couldn't help weeping solemn tears as he told O'Dessa he loved her with all his stupid heart and that his soul ached to know her, and would she have him, presumably as a husband.

He said this right in front of me and Robert. I stood sagging somewhat loudly between my companions, the Queen of Gypsies and the Nobleman. A moment of cold reality, like the dead clay chill of a fresh corpse a week old and stored up in a cellar, shrouded us all, including the Hoosier boy, or sort of fell over us gently as a cold sheet soaked in a snowfed river, like the Teslin, then left to dry on a wire suspended between spruce trees atop a mountain, then puffed up by a father and tucked under the chin and arms of his child. A mother has done the same . . .

But that passed, and O'Dessa let me go, and stepped past the college-bound boy to the trailer where Shorty tended Lord Byron when she and the Nobleman bathed me. She was gone a minute, searching, and when she came back with the Lord dead in her arms, her eyes hard as diamonds, she addressed the love-dead soul of the Hoosier boy, saying, "Where's the dwarf?"

The boy said a sheriff from South Dakota had come shortly before and arrested the dwarf under the charge of conspiracy to commit arson, and the success of that act, in the incineration of the school for wayward children in Meeganville. The headmaster and headmistress had perished.

The Hoosier lad reported these things now wholly sober and manly in his fate. He then walked down the road to where his companions were camped asleep in the gem-top camper, a red Ford F100 as I now recall. When he opened the window to climb into his bunk, one of them grumbled and he said nothing.

37

O'Dessa sat by lantern light, cradling the Lord in her arms. I had been hooked onto a tree, and hung there watching.

The dog had really meant little to me; since it was the ugliest creature God ever let breathe on its own on this earth, except perhaps for microscopic parasites living in the blood, hair, and skin, who vacate only after their host creatures are dead, and then only gradually. I felt a twinge of relief that we could bury him, burn him, or drop him in the river.

As I mulled this over, my head sank toward the lantern in fatigue, for baths always tired me, and Robert helped me lift my head back to rest against the tree . . .

For a brief time, it was utterly dead silent — not the sound of breathing nor the sighing of the mighty river in the deep vale below — but then Robert, now seated on the needle-strewn ground, began softly to mourn from his lungs and belly; a tune was made of the grinding and popping, and I have thought for a long time how to describe it. It sounded like corn popping in the bladder of a goat.

O'Dessa's black diamond eyes burnt up night like breathing opal hat pins; I could see them through my button eyes as river water wept in them from my hatless hair still wet from the river.

Robert went to the trees and vomited.

O'Dessa sighed like the river, and said, "These noblemen!" sitting upright on the stool like a ballerina. Then she hummed a tune, rocking the Lord whom she kissed under a black lace head-veil falling off the neck of a swan.

38

We buried Lord Byron in a green glass ten-gallon jug that had once held the fetus of a king. The label said, "Fetus of Giant Oceanic King."

Foresightedly, upon his capture Shorty had thrown his keys through the window of his truck. The Hoosier boy had told us. The keys, a great ring, had landed on the seat. We found them there. (I say "we," but I was a hanging witness.)

It was dawn before the Nobleman found the key that properly fit the back door of Shorty's truck trailer, and opened it. He carried the Coleman lantern up in there, and Dessa followed with the dog in her arms.

I saw rows of bottles on shelves as the Nobleman searched for a crypt. Locked in a private cabinet like a cherry clock-case at the back of the trailer, the Fetus of Giant Oceanic King was stored. Using all his might, the Nobleman snapped the padlocked bands engirdling the jug, and lifted it free of the casket.

For the first time in centuries, perhaps, the back of the cherry box glittered; it must've been painted black and dusted with gold glitter.

The Nobleman carried the jug outside and set it on the ground; first on a camp stool he'd set it, but the camp stool wavered without a set of human legs to hold it steady; then he set it on the ground. You could see pine needles through it, crushed by the weight . . .

A thick wire clamp held down the waxen-sealed dome-lid of the jar, and it took the Nobleman a half hour to figure out how to unclamp it using a foot-long screwdriver. Sweat poured down his red face and dripped off the tips of his moustache. The salty sweat ran off the round edges of the lid and down the emerald sides of the jar.

The container was on the ground about four feet from me, and right before he pried up the lid my feet began to shake so hard in my boots that my toes hit together. I drooled some kind of inert protestation in the green glass of the sacrilege, which I had not known was surfacing, and some ardent sounds erupted from my body and mouth — most like the horror-cries of a stroke victim, to tell you — for my bowels loosened and snot poured from my head of loose wires and tin whistles (where should have been the brain of a man!) as the Nobleman, using the screwdriver, prised up the lid and such an air of pickled corpse perked up whole as a ghost that he gasped and snorted and fell back kicking in the dirt of the Dreadnaught public arcade.

Wiser than us, the Queen stood by the trailer with Byron, up wind . . .

Finally, in a cloud of dirt and needles red, gray, green, copper, and brown, the frantic Nobleman's boot connected and toppled the jug, such that it fell like the clinking glass section of a once-Venetian tree or a mighty bell made of volcanic glass, into the arcadian dirt.

"My God!" I screamed. Dessa didn't move. The Nobleman spun backwards in the dirt like a faulty firework.

The liquid contents of the jar puddled the earth until the earth drank them up, but the king had not come out. The sea in which he had dwelt left him in there.

"No! O! God!" I screamed; t'was then I felt my teeth were gone. I wanted lifting off, and Dessa stepped forward. But not to lift me off the nail, no, for as she came my way she paused like someone finding a doll on the floor, and reached without air into the jug, took out the fetus and held it up to the sun which had risen over the dome of the pavillion.

39

Like one of those gunpowder snakes that melt and burn, he had looked. But after O'Dessa offered the Ocean King fetus to the sun, the Nobleman gentled down, and calm and complete or whole again in the morning light of the B.C. wilderness said: "I want an autopsy."

But Dessa wouldn't have it. I don't think she really heard him, so high she was in the pagan consecration. So with his eyes pressed shut, the Nobleman gripped up a fistful of wet soil where the juice had spilled, robbing the earth of a morsel in her ever-present maw, her sweet, salty, bitter lips that offer us so much, and pressed this mud to his face, rubbing it all over.

The mud hardened there as through the remaining hours of daylight Dessa and Bobby scoured the rig for whiskey sufficient to pickle the Lord.

40

The road from there out was tough, tainted with guilt, whereas it had been fairly joyous. It had been joyous and clean, if only weirdly animal.

You may recall the outset of this chronicle, my discussion through pictures of our whistle-stop Bible readings. Well, like Isaiah says, the old-day prophet, the rain will come. The rain muddies the mighty river and rinses the leaves of their dust.

Old John said it was the dust of time entering the river of time to form the body of time which we consume but cannot hold, then laughed. This came back to me last night in a sober dream. He had said, that night when I was stolen away, "You, straw man," laughter, "will be dissolved in the river, and your clodhoppers fished up by boys with cane poles." He meant the widow's gift.

"So, everything forms the body of time?" one of the boys who'd stolen me asked. That's when my real dream ended, and I fell back to sleep as memory crumbled.

41

It rained at the crucifixion, you know, as reported. It rained in the Bible.

42

We buried the King in the Teslin River but kept the Lord in the bottle. Everyone who paid their money to see Lord Byron of Newstead Abbey, the Dog Prince, thought they were seeing the Giant Fetus of the Oceanic King because we never took the original label off the bottle.

I say "we" though I was essentially a limber stiff, past my last leg, as I've tried to describe to you through my yo-yo life, ragged accouterements, and company of necessary attendants who put the finishing touches on my act when they hit me on the highway at Tin Cup, pitied me, patched me up, built me back and stuffed my limbs, even hayed my shoes so they would stay on, put a bird's nest in my hat which was lost in the Yukon River at Whitehorse, a dangerous venue, and fished up a buck off my corpse.

I've often wondered how different my life would be had I just stayed in my truck at Tin Cup. Very, I think.

43

Being toothless but vocal, I had to be careful. Even a scarecrow contains a spark of life, and I feared being dumped from the net some night in a river or, worse, burned in a shed-fire in case they got sick of my voice. Luckily, I had little to say.

Sometimes I felt like crying out when they hung me, sat me, or leaned me up somewhere within sight of their lovemaking. When this happened, I tried to dredge up memories of the children in the dream of farm life, or bits and snatches of Bible sayings, or Old John's laughter.

When jingling things lie loose in your head, they come back clearly but not by willpower, like gold coins deep in a well shining only when caught in a bucket, flushed up by a fish's tail or shoveled into the bucket by a crab. They could also be pennies in a farmhouse that rolled under the bed or the stove or the hutch, that children find when they are old, and children found when they were old, Old John said.

44

It got bad. I don't know why, exactly . . . It must've been they missed Shorty too much as someone who could hold the show together. Certainly, I was not born to sell tickets to my own show. Nor could a gypsy queen stand outside her tent, releasing all her mystery for free. And the illiterate Nobleman had insufficient vocabulary, a dearth of confidence.

Sometimes the smell of incense and cedar was so strong from Shorty's truck passing through town with its back doors tied open that a few folks with olfactory systems strong enough to stir curiosity and drag them from their homes would come around when we parked outside the city limits. (This was called the Nose Hook in the Old World, and freaks among us know.) But the smell ploy didn't work on still days, or days in Saskatchewan and the flat provinces where the four winds eradicate all fragrance . . .

But it wasn't just bad because people stopped coming. We could've gotten by on what we made. It had to be they missed Shorty too much as somebody who held things together with the glue of his earnest wish to help the weird

bubbles flowing from their mouths (which opened at his jawbones) became the bright dots that outlined the rivery creases.

She pierced his eyeball one time, due to fatigue; he screamed from sleep and his eyeball turned the whole red of blood, his own blood, but Dessa shouted, "Whoopee! The blood of the Snake!" and laughed as Bobby rolled on the ground.

"The blood of the Rose!" she shouted, and he calmed down. Then they made love before me . . .

Before she let him release, she pierced the other eye through the lid, for symmetry. As he screamed, grimacing, he released . . .

You know what the tender language means, gauze through which the gore-blood oozes . . .But you know, you see it . . . It is on the picnic table by the road. In fact, when Dessa became with child Bobby carved their initials on a picnic table. Then they mixed their blood in a bowl and dyed the heart made of two snakes with mouths and tails joined, surrounded by a nest of roses. Somewhere in Alberta. Alberta Beach, Alberta . . .

When it got so bad, I partook of the black aspirin and, deprived of dreams day after day for days on end where you lose track of sunrises and fail to eat the gruel they serve to the toothless rag you've become, unable to protest being hung on a tree for fear of fire or the river, I knew I had to escape.

Yet I knew this was impossible. My knees barely worked to lift my feet when I hung from the tree, and I could not imagine lifting them, shoes and all, if on the ground I tried to walk under the sack of all my weight!

46

It was six months into her pregnancy and a cold night in August when we pulled into Whitehorse. By now, Bobby was completely tattoo'd, such that no white skin showed. His head and moustache were shaved, you couldn't tell he was blonde, and the soles of his feet were tattoo'd red to look like thorns were broken off in them — like a man who ran through thistles and briars from a witch, a bull, or the Tar Baby.

His feet formed the most intricately conceived, painstakingly executed "tat" I'd ever seen. Depicted on the arch, peeking over the bridge of each foot, troll children (more green than red, more brownie than troll — a race hard to nab) saw the featureless Babe chase the Red Bull, while on t'other foot the Witch ran. She covered the whole top of one foot, with her tree of hair, her dress in her hands. She could have been just a beautiful girl running from a bull and a babe, but when Bobby flexed his feet you saw the eyes and mouth widen wild to feed on the two she chased.

Bob had had his toenails removed by a podiatrist in Corn Center (where Old John rented me), Idaho, where Shorty had shut down the show for a night. He'd had his toenails removed so that the skin beneath them could be utilized for the act. On those surfaces, O'Dessa had tattoo'd little hands clapping under little faces containing the various emotions: fear, hate, envy, love, courage, faith, hope, regret, and despair. The little toe on Bobby's left foot had been lost in a crusade, he told when asked . . .

Bobby's ears were tattoo'd black so that against his dark green reptilian skull they almost couldn't be seen, and in the cave of each ear O'Dessa had placed a red star. From a distance the stars looked like ladybugs and drew a great deal of attention, stirring in the onlooker a feeling of great irritation, making his fingers move and eyes water. I have heard that only one act at a time in the world can produce this.

47

You hear lots of lies on the road with a freak show. I told one yesterday, that Corn Center's in Idaho. It grew like a weed up my leg, through the darkness of my clothing.

Who knows when it was planted? Did it blow in through the window of the truck? Did it float to me on gypsy music? Was it in the gunpowder tea? Did a farmboy or shepherdess slip it in my pocket with a dollar or coin, where it rotted in the mulch and fell down my pants leg to my shoe?

I only know the general time period in which the lie was born. I was King of Scarecrows and thirty-one years old.

48

We camped outside Whitehorse at a little place called Mosquito Creek, aptly named as it turns out. We couldn't stay in Whitehorse proper because, even that far north in the territory, they had put a ban on freak shows.

It seems a decade before, a geek from Texas had choked to death responding to a hundred-dollar wager he couldn't swallow the mayor's rat in so many seconds without aid. I'm not sure if this was the mayor of the capitol or some outlying community.

Anyhow, the geek's family down in Fate tried to extradite the mayor for the murder of their sole provider, Winston. They figured the mayor of a town in gold country must have some dough, Big Rita said, but the only dough he had was sourdough.

Big Rita was the matron of the town where we ended up parking Shorty's rig amid a thicket of pine trees — *grove* is the proper word — where Wolf Creek meets Mosquito Creek and both flow into a bog.

A big crow, the biggest I'd ever laid eyes on, worked for Rita there, scaring honeymooners, poor tourists, societal misfits, and freaks who camped at Big Rita's Lodge. People with more money stayed in the lodge, which was a combo cafe/bar/gas station and shower house, where you put coins in a scummy slot in the knob attached to a wall you had to turn to the number of minutes you paid for, but inside the lodge proper the rich had private shower baths with ever-lasting water.

Rita had the world by the tail. People of our genre couldn't stay overnight in Whitehorse, and you couldn't bathe in or partake of either creek that died nearby. Rita had the only combination cafe/bar/gas station outside Whitehorse for sixty miles.

On the second morning we were there (I had been left outside the truck, and was asleep against a pine tree, seated on a thick mat of straw), I saw the big crow — which was a loner and had no mate — peck, peck, peck, peck, peck the side of a little pup tent where two honeymooners slept.

The giggling girl, curiously evicted, crawled out of the tent as the animal gaggled a sort of wicked laugh.

I saw what was coming, but she wouldn't look my way.

"Oh, Jasper, look! Come out! See this crow!"

As she so beseeched her husband, the bride reached for the bird to pet it; it had hopped onto the peak of the tent; it pecked at her hand; she jerked back and laughed.

"Jasper, bring some bread!"

When Jasper offered the bread to the bird, it screamed "Get out! Get out! Get out! You fiend! You fiend! You fiend!" and the boy and girl laughed. Then the animal leapt onto Jasper's arm and up it to his shoulder. It pecked his eye; he shrieked and fell rolling to the earth, the bag of bread in his hand, the giant bird attached as firmly to his thicket of young black hair as a tick to a dog.

I moved a little till I slid from the trunk, but O'Dessa ran out naked as a jaybird and kicked the beast off the honeymooner's bloody mane.

The bride wept hysterical as the completely naked Nobleman comforted her and led her for medicine to the tent, where "the goose was warm" — meaning the goosedown bag, while the Queen of Gypsies nursed the bloody Jasper.

49

Turns out Jasper was a juggler. By nightfall he'd juggled everything liftable in camp.

Big Rita, who'd seen everything from her office window, came down from the lodge bearing a gift of a small Pecos watermelon which, in those days, sold for a dollar a pound, approximately, in Whitehorse, Dawson, Tok, Esther, or Fairbanks. She told us no watermelons edible were available north of Fairbanks after August fifteenth. I didn't know how she could know this, really, Alaska and the Canada surroundant being so vast, and her being stuck for all practical purposes at the lodge, but she wasn't so much talking to me as to O'Dessa, whom she wanted to stay on as a "hostess curio" at the lodge which she told us point blank she was planning to "doll up" and change the character of completely.

Dessa seemed attracted extraordinarily, but what about Bobby Topanga, she wondered aloud.

"Well," Rita said, looking at the completely naked, illuminated man, "what can you do?"

Bobby was buffaloed and ignorant; embarrassed, he shook his head and retreated to the trailer, where he and Dessa shared the Murphy bunk.

"He can't read," Dessa told her, "and he never applied for a job."

Rita, who'd really been around, said, "That explains a lot." Then, very sincerely, and gazing after the Nobleman as if the shifting pair of painted tortoises tattoo'd on his buttocks still were there, she said: "He lives in a world of pictures."

50

I had not planned to go this far, but I guess I should, since I know all too well what it feels like to be left hanging . . .

Bobby stayed on as bartender at Rita's lodge which she called Engelmann Lodge after all the renovations were complete.

Bobby and Dessa sold the rig to Jasper and Jasper's wife whom Dessa instructed without pay in the arts of the gypsy, primarily fortunetelling.

Jasper's mother and father had purchased a life insurance policy on his life when he was born and they gave it to Jasper and his new bride as a wedding present. In turn, Jasper cashed the policy and paid for the carnival rig. I think it was $10,000 . . .

Jasper and his wife headed south. As a belated wedding gift and apology for what happened at the lodge, as if it weren't fate, Rita coaxed the giant crow into a golden cage and locked the cage and gave it with a signed certificate to Jasper and his wife to add to the store of curiosities already acquired through the purchase of the truck and all its contents.

We used to sit around the lodge and wonder aloud about what Jasper and the woman's new name for the Weirdest World on Wheels might be. After buying the vehicle, the raven-haired Quebecker volunteered quite confidently that he was going to paint it green and change the name since "Shorty Longhorn is dead."

I knew better, of course, but feared sharing my knowledge with a juggler, though of all people a juggler of watermelons, Indian clubs, pickled preciosities, and snakes should be trusted to know how everything balances out which falls to earth. Even the stars fall to earth as we have seen them . . .

I didn't. Instead, I watched the comings and goings of carpenters and decorators imported from far away, from the vantage point of a bench in the foyer where Rita set me. It was not a bad life, holding my tongue between my gums, and then between the teeth she bought me. I even learned to grin in a certain way. It was a good job, the kind of employment you just can't hardly find if you go out looking for it.

It got to the point, too, that Rita paid me something for my efforts, and people left money in my hands that stayed in my pockets that Rita made new, and under my bunk in the hothouse I found a box of moldy Gideons which I smuggled to the lodge in my vestments.